PURRFECT DECEIT

THE MYSTERIES OF MAX 32

NIC SAINT

PURRFECT DECEIT

The Mysteries of Max 32

Copyright © 2021 by Nic Saint

Edited by Chereese Graves

www.nicsaint.com

Give feedback on the book at: info@nicsaint.com

facebook.com/nicsaintauthor
@nicsaintauthor

First Edition

Printed in the U.S.A

*W*e were in Odelia's office doing what we do best: having a refreshing nap. Not that napping is all we do, mind you. Sometimes we doze, and sometimes we even sleep. Dooley and I occupied one corner of the office, Harriet and Brutus another. Recently a sort of disagreement had broken out between the two factions that make up Odelia's cat contingent and I can only blame The Wedding for this frankly embarrassing fracas.

A wedding had taken place in Las Vegas, and Odelia and Chase Kingsley had officially been declared husband and wife. It had been one of those shotgun weddings, though fortunately no shotguns had featured into the thing, and a good thing, too, I should say.

The moment we returned from Vegas however, two things happened that caused a kind of rift: first off, a great number of people who'd heard through the grapevine about the wedding were vocally displeased, and didn't mind expressing this displeasure to one and all. As Odelia's cats we more or less bore the brunt of this displeasure, as our fellow felines in the local community turned to us to tell of their annoyance with the way the whole thing had gone down, and this naturally weighed on all of our minds.

Harriet, fed up with all this criticism, which she felt she didn't deserve, figured Dooley and I were mostly to blame, as we should have used our influence to discourage Odelia from going through with her plan, even though at the time Harriet had thought it was a great idea—something she'd since conveniently forgotten, I might add.

And then there was the second dispute that soured things to some extent.

"The stork, Max!" said Dooley. "It's the stork! I can see him! Quick, let's catch him before he takes off again!"

I looked in the direction indicated but unfortunately didn't see any sign of said stork.

"Um… I'm afraid I don't see any stork, Dooley," I said therefore.

He stared at the window, through which a sliver of blue sky was visible. "Oh," he said finally. "I thought I saw it. Must have been some other bird."

"Will you please shut up about your stork," Harriet yelled from her side of the room.

"Yeah, some of us are trying to take a quiet nap," Brutus chimed in.

"I'm sorry," said Dooley. "It's just that… you know how important it is, you guys. And I think we should all be on the lookout for that stork twenty-four seven."

"You be on the lookout," said Harriet. "Brutus and I have better things to do."

"We could take shifts," Dooley suggested, turning a hopeful face to me. "I could watch out while you take a nap, and you could watch out while I take a nap. And vice versa?"

"Sure, Dooley," I said reassuringly. "Don't you worry about a thing. You take your nap and I'll make sure that stork doesn't pass by this office without me attracting its attention and making sure it does what it's supposed to do."

"And what's that?" asked Brutus. "Take a dump and fly off again?" He seemed to think his joke was very funny, for he suddenly broke into uproarious laughter.

"You know how important this is, Brutus," said Dooley, sounding a little hurt. "If we don't catch that stork, Odelia will never have her baby, and then she'll be very sad."

"Oh, Dooley," said Harriet with a sigh, even as Brutus shook his head.

"What?" said Dooley. "It's true, though, isn't it? This is very, very important."

"Absolutely, Dooley," I said with a smile. As long as Dooley was on the lookout for the stork delivering Odelia's baby there was no need for me to go into all that birds and bees stuff again, something I thoroughly dislike, I don't mind telling you.

"What are you guys talking about?" asked Odelia, busily typing at her computer.

"Oh, nothing special," I said, and Dooley gave me a fat wink.

So you can probably see what the issue was, can't you: ever since we got back from Vegas, Dooley has been very anxious about the baby he was sure was about to land any moment now, courtesy of that mysterious stork. He'd pretty much equated marriage with the arrival of a bundle of joy from the heavens, and since Odelia was so incredibly busy all the time, he was afraid she'd miss the stork's arrival and her chance at having a baby—or two.

Harriet and Brutus, on the other hand, weren't all that excited at the prospect of an addition to the family, though in all honesty it was mostly Harriet who was very vocal in expressing her views on the subject. Not when Odelia could hear her, mind you. The last thing she wanted was to antagonize our human and cause that incessant flow of kibble to suddenly dry up, something that was entirely Odelia's prerogative, of course.

A knock at the door sounded, and when we looked up we saw that a man had arrived sporting an anxious look on his face.

"Miss Poole?" he said hesitantly. "Miss Odelia Poole?"

"Yep, that's me," said Odelia, looking up from her computer. "What can I do for you?"

The man hesitantly entered the office and took a seat across from the intrepid reporter. He was a man in his early thirties I would have guessed, a little thin on top, who wore thick-framed glasses and had a mephistophelian beard going on. The kind of beard Robert Downey Jr. rocks when he's flying around dressed as a man of iron. Unfortunately while such a beard becomes Mr. Downey well, it didn't do much for this man's doughy face and pasty pallor. Then again, we can't all be Hollywood stars, now can we?

"A friend of mine said you're the person to talk to when some delicate issue crops up," the man said, after shuffling back and forth on his chair for a few beats, while Odelia patiently waited for him to launch into an explanation for why he'd decided to intrude upon her precious time.

"A delicate issue?" asked Odelia, frowning slightly. "What delicate issue, Mr…"

"Curtis," said the man. "Joshua Curtis. Um…" He glanced around, as if to make sure they wouldn't be disturbed, and conveniently ignored all four of us, dismissing us as not relevant, as most humans do. He scooted a little forward on his chair, then said, "Can I rely on your absolute discretion, Miss Poole? This is, as I said, a matter of the utmost delicacy."

"Yes, of course," said Odelia. She gave the man a smile intended to put him at ease. "While I'm not an attorney, and I can't fall back on the old client confidentiality thing…"

"Or a priest," I muttered.

"I will of course treat whatever you want to tell me with the necessary discretion."

Mr. Curtis nodded, then seemed to screw up his courage and said, "A friend of mine is in trouble, Miss Poole."

"Just call me Odelia," said our fair-haired human who, last I checked, was as svelte as she's always been, which meant that in spite of Dooley's ministrations no baby bump was growing. She flashed more of that encouraging smile of hers at the man, the smile that makes people in all walks of life entrust her with their deepest confidences.

"The thing is, Jason and I have been best friends since college, see. And since he got married I like to think that his wife Melanie and I have also become very close friends."

"Are you yourself married, Joshua?" asked Odelia, as a way to break the ice.

"Um, no, as a matter of fact I'm not," said the man, nervously rubbing his hands on his trousers. "I came close," he quickly added with a weak smile, "but no luck so far."

"So your friend Jason is in some kind of trouble?"

"Yes, well, actually his wife Melanie is. She…" Mr. Curtis took another deep breath. "The thing is, Melanie's been seeing someone."

"You mean, someone other than her husband?"

Joshua nodded. "I'm afraid so."

"Does your friend know about this?"

"Pretty sure that he doesn't. And frankly I'd like to keep it that way. See the thing is… Jason and Melanie mean a lot to me, Miss Poo—Odelia. I consider them more than friends. They're like family, and their happiness is very important to me."

"Have you talked to Melanie about this?"

"No. No, I haven't. I'm afraid that if I do… See, the thing

is that I'm not a hundred percent sure." He shrugged. "Maybe I'm seeing things. But I don't think so."

"Why do you think she's having an affair?"

"It all started two weeks ago. Jason told me that Melanie had started working late, and that he was worried about her. He felt she was taking on too much. And so he asked me to talk to her. Maybe convince her to talk to her boss about rearranging her workload some."

"And what did she say?"

"The thing is," said Joshua, looking a little embarrassed, "that I thought the best thing would be for me to have a talk with Melanie's boss myself. You see, Melanie and I used to be colleagues once upon a time, and her boss used to be my boss, too. So I just figured I'd have a friendly little chat with him at his local hangout, which happens to be my local hangout, too. Only when I told him to cut Melanie some slack, he was surprised. Said Melanie's workload hasn't changed. No overtime, no nothing. She clocks in and out like she's always done. Actually he'd noticed the opposite: she's been clocking out early the last couple of weeks, and taking longer lunch breaks."

"Which of course made you wonder where she'd been spending those hours she claimed she was working late," Odelia said, nodding.

Joshua cleared his throat. "I would have asked Melanie about it, but I really don't want to ruin a beautiful friendship, and I don't want her to think I'm spying on her. So…" He gave Odelia a hopeful look.

Odelia smiled. "You want me to find out what your friend's wife's been up to."

"I'll pay you, of course," said Joshua quickly, taking out his wallet.

Odelia held up her hand. "I don't know what you've heard, but I'm not a private detective, Joshua. I'm a reporter."

"Oh, I know you're a reporter. But my friend told me you're also an ace detective—probably the only detective in town. So…"

Odelia settled back for a moment, and cast a glance in my direction. I gave her a thoughtful nod. She was, indeed, a grade-A sleuth, and why shouldn't she earn an extra buck if people wanted to avail themselves of her obvious talents? Besides, now that she was married she probably could use the extra money. Contrary to what you might think reporters don't exactly make the big bucks, and neither do small-town cops. And even if no stork flew in through the window and deposited a newborn on her couch, she still had four extra mouths to feed, so basically I was just looking out for yours truly!

"All right," she said at length. "Here's what I'll do. I'll talk it over with my boss. See if he thinks it's a good idea. And I'll let you know as soon as I decide. How does that sound?"

"That sounds excellent," said Joshua, looking much relieved. "Though I have to tell you that this is a matter of some urgency, as my friend told me just this morning that Melanie told him she's got another late night scheduled for tonight."

"I'll see what I can do," said Odelia, continuing to be noncommittal, even though I could tell that she was intrigued, and eager to take the case and look into this matter.

"*D*an, I need to ask you something."

Odelia's boss Dan Goory, senior—and only—editor of the Hampton Cove Gazette, looked up from the perusal of his own newspaper, and gave his senior—and only—reporter a quick glance. "Don't tell me you finally wrote that tell-all article about your Vegas wedding?"

Odelia grimaced. "I'll never write that article, Dan. I told you that."

"But people are waiting to read all about it, honey. Warts and all." He grinned, his white beard waggling invitingly. "In fact the more warts the better, you know that."

"There was nothing especially exciting about my wedding, Dan. We flew down there, got married, had dinner, and that's it. Shortest and least glamorous wedding in history."

"Come on," he goaded her. "There must be something. Pictures of your grandmother completely drunk and dancing on top of the table? Or your dad hitting the slot machines and making a killing—or the slot machines killing him?"

"Nothing happened, Dan. Nothing worth reading about."

Her editor shrugged his shoulders, and a frown slid across his aged features. "Look, if you don't want to talk about it, that's fine. What did you want to see me about?"

His tone had taken on a more official note, a note she didn't like. She heaved a silent sigh. Ever since she'd returned from Vegas people had been acting a little weird, and she knew exactly why that was. The list of wedding guests had been extremely short: only Odelia's and Chase's immediate family and friends, and no one else. And quite a few people in her circle were still upset that they hadn't been included in the festivities.

"I just had a guy come in who wants me to look into the alleged affair of his best friend's wife," she said, taking a seat in front of her boss's desk. "Only problem is..."

"You're not a private investigator," he said tersely. "You're a reporter and so you have no business taking on clients and investigating their cases."

"Yeah, that's about the gist of it," she admitted. She'd hoped Dan would be encouraging. That he would say, 'Of course, Odelia—go for it! Investigate away!' Instead he regarded her a little coldly. "So look, I didn't want to take the case without discussing it with you first. So this is me, discussing it with you."

"Well, we've discussed it," said Dan, leaning back in his chair and steepling his fingers. "And I have to tell you I don't think this is a good idea, Odelia. You're not a licensed investigator... What happens if you get hurt in the course of this investigation? You're not insured. You're not protected. There are reasons why private detectives have to get a license and have to take out insurance. You can't just go around pretending to be a detective like some overage Nancy Drew." He must have seen the dismay she clearly felt for being called an overage Nancy Drew, for he suddenly softened, those harsh lines in his face smoothing out. "Look, I'm sorry," he said. "I know that you're an ace sleuth, licensed or not licensed, and I also know that your reputation is spreading through this community like wildfire, so more and more people will find their way to your doorstep—or your office door..." He paused, then seemed to relent. "Why is this guy—"

"Joshua Curtis," she quickly supplied.

"Why is Joshua Curtis so eager to ascertain whether his friend's wife is having an affair? What business is it to him? She's not his wife."

"He feels protective of his friend, I guess. He happened to find out that the guy's wife is lying and now he wants to figure out what's going on."

"Why doesn't he simply talk to her about it?"

"He's afraid to. Afraid she'll get upset. Also, he's not sure."

"I see."

"So he figures if I dig around a little, and maybe snap a couple of shots, he's got proof. And she won't be able to dismiss him when he does finally confront her."

"Okay, so suppose she is having an affair, and that you do get this... photographic evidence of these illicit fumblings behind her husband's back. Then what?"

"Like I said, he'll confront her with the evidence, and tell her that if she doesn't stop the affair he'll tell her husband."

Dan thought about this for a moment. "Look, I know Joshua. And I know how close he and Jason Myers are."

"You know these guys?" She shouldn't have been surprised. Dan probably knew everyone in Hampton Cove. That's what happened when you published a weekly paper for over forty years.

"Oh, sure. I remember when they were little, Jason used to get into all kinds of trouble, and Joshua would then try to get him out of it. They were like brothers, those two."

"Still are, from what I understand."

Dan leaned forward. "What surprises me is Melanie having an affair. She doesn't seem like the type."

"Do you have to be a certain type to have an affair?" asked Odelia a little ironically.

"Well, yeah, I think so. Take you, for instance. I can tell you for a fact that you will never cheat on your husband, and neither will your husband ever cheat on you."

"Well, that's a relief," she quipped.

He quirked a bushy white eyebrow. "I'm being serious here, Odelia. It's human psychology. You and Chase simply aren't wired that way."

"And Melanie Myers isn't either?"

"I didn't think so. Though if what you're saying is true, then obviously I was wrong. Maybe my mischief radar isn't as tuned as well as I thought."

"So what do you think, boss? Do I take the case or not?" She eagerly awaited his response. She enjoyed these infrequent forays into the world of sleuthing, though if Dan told her to say no, she would. He was, after all, the boss. The guy paying the bills.

"Do you see a story in there?" he asked.

"Um…"

He shrugged. "Just say yes. If Melanie really is having an affair behind her husband's back, maybe it's a good thing that Joshua is watching out for his friend. If nothing else we can always use it for our Dear Gabi column."

A wide smile spread across Odelia's face. "Thanks, Dan," she said, getting up. "You won't regret it."

"And get busy on that article about your wedding!" he called after her. "I want to see pictures of your grandma completely plastered and so does everyone else in Hampton Cove!"

I don't know if you've ever been an assistant private sleuth? You haven't? I can tell you right now that you haven't missed much. Basically what sleuths do is sit in their cars and spy on people. Mostly people being unfaithful to their spouse. And then they try to take pictures of this act of adultery, as I think the technical term is, and show it to the husband or wife. Though in this case, I guess, we were doing things a little differently, as the photographic proof of Mrs. Myers's infidelity would not go to her husband but to her husband's childhood friend.

And so it was that we were following Mrs. Myers around for the better portion of the day, and making sure we were in a position to catch her in the act. Odelia had picked her up as she left the house—and a very nice house it was, too, and one she would probably stand to lose if she kept up this infidelity thing—and then we trailed her all through town. Which basically meant we tailed her to the real estate agency where she worked as a broker, and sat there twiddling our thumbs for the better part of the morning.

At one point Odelia had ventured inside, just to make

sure our quarry was still present and accounted for, and hadn't fled through the backdoor for some secret canoodling. But Melanie Myers had still been at her desk. In fact she'd been the one to join Odelia at the reception desk and ask her if she was in the market for a house. She'd of course immediately recognized Odelia as a new bride, and chatting had ensued.

"Oh, God," said Odelia the moment she let herself tumble down into her car seat, "I'm probably the worst private detective in the world. What was I thinking, going in there? Now she's seen my face and when she sees me next she'll know I'm following her around!"

"What did she say?" I asked. "Does she know you're tailing her?"

"I don't think so," said Odelia with a shake of the head. "She asked me a lot of questions about the wedding, and wanted to know what dress I wore and all that guff."

"She's not one of those people who are mad with you for not inviting them to the wedding, is she?" asked Harriet.

"No, I don't think she was invited. Though maybe she was. In the end there were so many people inviting themselves I have no idea who was and who wasn't!" She rubbed her face. "Maybe I should do a course. Sleuthing for dummies or something. I'm sure there are tricks of the trade I should master before I put myself out there like this."

"You're doing great," said Dooley, who always likes to take a positive view of things.

"Thanks for the vote of confidence, Dooley," said Odelia as she glanced through the windshield at the real estate agency across the street. It was called 'wefindyourdreamhomeforyou.com' and was a popular place, with plenty of customers walking in and out, and others stopping to do some window shopping. "At least now I know she's still in there and not in some hotel or motel with her suspected lover boy."

"Who is this lover boy?" asked Harriet, who was very interested in this case, I felt. But then Harriet is really into things like The Bachelor and The Bachelorette, and I guess infidelity and relationship issues are part and parcel of those types of dating shows.

"I have absolutely no idea," said Odelia. "And as far as I could tell Joshua doesn't have any idea either. Which is probably why he hired me: to find out who this guy is."

"If he even exists," I said.

"Oh, he exists, all right," said Harriet. "Did you see the woman's face? She looks much too happy. I'd say she's been having a torrid affair for quite some time. No married person ever looks this happy."

Odelia slowly turned to face the prissy Persian. "I'm a married person. Are you saying I don't look happy?"

"Oh, but you just got married," said Harriet quickly. "Newlyweds always look happy. It's when they've been married for a while that the problems begin."

Odelia was frowning. A new bride doesn't like to be reminded that marriage problems exist, let alone are a contingency to watch out for. "Pray tell, Harriet."

"Well, obviously I can't speak from experience," Harriet began.

"Obviously."

"But from what I've seen, the problems usually begin when babies enter the picture. I think you'd do well to consider putting off any ideas of a family expansion in the immediate future. In fact I think having babies is the best way to guarantee the end of that blissful honeymoon stage you're enjoying so much right now."

"And how do you figure that?" asked Odelia, who didn't

look entirely convinced by Harriet's unbidden marriage advice.

"Well, babies drive a wedge between husband and wife, see. I don't know if you've noticed but babies cry. In fact crying is pretty much all they do. They cry at night, they cry during the day, and all this crying makes it so that mom and dad never get a minute of sleep. So this makes them cranky, as most humans need a lot of sleep. And that's when the shouting begins, and the recriminations, and before long the D word is dropped."

"The D word?" asked Dooley. "You don't mean… Drugs!"

"I was actually thinking about Divorce, but drugs might be a factor," Harriet said, nodding. "So you see? Better don't start a family, Odelia. Besides, babies are overrated, and with overpopulation and stuff I think it's wise to simply drop the whole idea."

"Oh, Harriet," said Odelia with a laugh. "You're like a walking, talking contraception ad."

Harriet, who clearly felt this was praise of the highest order, beamed. "Thank you!"

"I think you should start with babies very soon," said Dooley, countering Harriet's gloomy view. "In fact I'm keeping an eye out for that stork for you, Odelia, and the moment I see him I'm flagging him down, don't you worry."

"I'm not worried, Dooley," said Odelia with a half-smile as she gave my friend a pat on the head. "But between you and me," she added, leaning in and dropping her voice to a whisper, "babies are the furthest thing from my mind right now."

"Good!" Harriet cried. "Excellent! I suggest you keep it that way!"

"But Odelia!" said Dooley. "What if the stork comes? What do I tell him?"

"You tell him—" Odelia started to say, but whatever Dooley was supposed to tell the stork would have to wait, as just at that moment Melanie Myers came walking out of the agency, swinging a mean purse, sashaying in the direction of Main Street.

"Max, Dooley, Harriet, Brutus!" Odelia snapped. "Follow that woman!"

4

*O*delia had opened the door and so we jumped out of the car and hurried to follow that woman, and not let her out of our sight even for one second!

"I don't understand, Max," said Dooley as he panted a little from the exertion. "Why doesn't Odelia follow her? Doesn't she want to take pictures when she meets the boyfriend?"

"Oh, Odelia is following her," I assured my friend. And when we both glanced back we saw that indeed our human was following at some distance, making sure she wasn't getting too close. On the other side of the street, meanwhile, Harriet and Brutus had also taken up the pursuit. So now no less than five operatives were on the case! Good thing four of those operatives were paid in kibble, or else this operation would get costly!

"It would probably be a good thing if in the future Odelia outfitted us with some kind of tracking device," I said, "or a hot mic through which we could all communicate. I think that's how the professionals do things when they're in surveillance mode."

"I don't think I'd like it if Odelia gave me a hot mic," said Dooley. "I think it would get very hot against my skin, and I don't like hot things pressing against my skin."

"A hot mic isn't actually hot, Dooley," I explained. "They just call it a hot mic because it's recording all the time."

"Oh. Then I guess it's fine. She can give me a hot mic, so I can tell her when I see the stork." He raised his eyes to the heavens to show me what he meant. Though apparently no storks were in evidence just then, for he kept his tongue, hot mic or not.

As luck would have it, Melanie Myers walked into the hair salon, and since the hairdresser's cat Buster is a close friend, our operative force had just expanded to six!

Dooley and I immediately set paw inside, and slunk into a corner where we took up our vigil, remaining as inconspicuous as a blorange cat of sizable proportions and his gray ragamuffin friend can be. We shouldn't have worried, though, for Melanie wasn't the least bit interested in us—or the rest of her surroundings. In fact the moment she took a seat in the waiting area, and picked up a copy of Cosmo, her phone jangled and she expertly fished it out of her purse with long fingernails and clicked it to life.

"She's very pretty," said Dooley as he stared at our target admiringly. And indeed Mrs. Myers was very pretty. She had that statuesque thing down pat, and her sense of dress was very elegant and chic. If a woman like Melanie showed me a house, I'm pretty sure I'd immediately say yes and snap it up at any price she wanted for it. Though of course as a cat it's hard to buy a house since we rarely carry any money on our person or even have a bank account, for that matter. Plus, banks are hesitant to give us a mortgage.

"Hello, darling," Melanie purred into her phone as she turned her face to the window and stared out. She'd lowered her voice, and had added that sexy tone that some men like so much. "Are you ready for tonight?" she asked. She listened for a moment, and I could see her face fall. Evidently the person on the other end wasn't ready for tonight, for she said sharply, "You have got to be kidding me." There was more talking on the other end, though obviously I couldn't hear what was being said, but Melanie's face had taken on a look of consternation, so clearly things weren't going according to plan. "Are you breaking up with me?" she asked, a sudden quiver in her voice. "Is that what this is?" And I guess that was exactly what this was, for a few moments later she said, very quietly, "Bye," and lowered her phone, then just sat there for a moment, still gazing out of that window, but this time with what are usually termed unseeing eyes.

I even thought I detected a tear that had formed in the eye that was visible from where I sat, and Dooley said, "What is happening, Max?"

"I think her boyfriend just dumped her, Dooley," I said.

"Oh, so that's a good thing, right?"

"Melanie doesn't seem to think so."

But then Fido Siniawski summoned her to take place in one of his chairs, and Melanie pulled herself together with an extreme effort and stalked over, head held high.

❧

*R*eturning to the office, Odelia felt a sense of disappointment. When you're all geared up to tackle a problem, and the problem simply yields all by itself, the end result can be disconcerting. Not unlike putting your foot down expecting that one final step and discovering you've already reached the ground floor. It's jarring, to say the least.

But since she'd been asked to do a job, she decided not to overthink things. Joshua Curtis had asked her for results, and clearly she'd been able to get the results desired. So she picked up her phone and put in the call.

Joshua picked up on the first ring. "Yes, Miss Poole? What have you discovered?"

"Well, it would appear that your friend was dumped by her boyfriend," said Odelia.

"Dumped? What do you mean?"

"He called her while she was at the hair salon," she explained. "And dumped her over the phone. Apparently they were supposed to meet up but instead he said it was over."

"Huh," said Joshua, clearly as taken aback by this denouement as Odelia herself was. "He dumped her over the phone? The bastard," he said with some heat.

"Yeah, she looked devastated," said Odelia, transferring the information Max and Dooley had gleaned from their surveillance. "I don't think she was expecting it."

"Poor Melanie," said Joshua. "So do you know who the guy is yet?"

"No, I don't. Do you still want me to keep going? I mean, the affair, if there ever was one, seems to be over. So there really is no point in bringing it up with her, I guess."

"No, I guess not," Joshua agreed. "Just… just to satisfy my curiosity, though, Miss Poole, could you maybe find out who the guy is? Just in case she resumes the affair. And take plenty of pictures, if you can. I want some good shots of the evil bastard."

It sounded like a fair enough request, Odelia thought, so she said, "Sure thing, Joshua. I'll try to find out. Though now that the affair is over, that might prove a lot harder."

"See what you can do," he said, and disconnected.

Odelia swiveled in her chair for a moment, thinking up ways and means of figuring out who this mystery man could possibly be.

5

*T*his was probably the shortest case in the history of cases," said Dooley.

"Yeah, it sure was," I agreed.

"And we solved it, Max!"

"We didn't solve anything, Dooley," I said. "The case more or less solved itself."

"I don't get it," said Harriet. "This is an attractive woman, and this guy simply dumps her? And over the phone, no less? If I were her I'd press charges."

"You can't press charges against a man you're having an affair with, Harriet," I pointed out.

"Yeah, if she presses charges her husband will find out," Brutus said. "And I don't think that's what she wants."

"But he can't just treat her like that!" said Harriet, all the female in her annoyed.

"Poor Melanie," said Dooley. "She looked very sad, didn't she?"

"She sure did," I said.

After having been dismissed by Odelia, we operatives found nothing better to do than to wander around a little aimlessly in downtown Hampton Cove. That's what operatives do, you know: they live for the chase, but when the chase is over, all that adrenaline that's been coursing through their system needs to settle down, and it makes you feel a little bit on edge. Just like soldiers who've been fighting several tours of duty and then arrive home to a sedentary life. Though probably I'm stretching the comparison a little.

We'd arrived at the General Store, where I saw that our friend Kingman was holding court on the sidewalk as usual.

"Hey, you guys!" he shouted by way of greeting. "Wilbur is still pretty upset with you. So if I were you I wouldn't let him see you."

"Indeed? Why is he upset with us?" asked Harriet.

"Because he wasn't invited to the wedding, of course!" said Kingman. "In fact there's a whole lot of very angry people in Hampton Cove right now!"

"But we can't help it if Odelia decided to cancel the wedding," I said. "It was her decision, not ours. So why do we have to suffer?"

"Wilbur wouldn't chase us away," said Brutus. "He knows it's not our fault."

But we still made sure to glance in Wilbur's direction, and make sure that if he did come after us, our exit strategy was in place.

"So how did it go?" asked Kingman eagerly.

"We solved the case in less than ten minutes!" said Dooley proudly.

"What case? I was talking about the wedding."

"Oh, the wedding" said Dooley, as if Kingman was referring to some old news.

"Yeah, the wedding!" said Kingman, sounding a little peeved himself, to be honest. "The wedding we were all invited to, and were all looking forward to, and then all of a sudden it was canceled and now we don't even get to see pictures! Or silly videos!"

"Oh, there are pictures," said Harriet.

"And silly videos," Brutus added.

"But Odelia is not going to put them on the Gazette website."

"Or her social media."

"She's not?" asked Kingman, looking surprised. "But... isn't she obliged to publish that stuff? She is a reporter, isn't she? Isn't there a law about that kind of thing?"

"A reporter isn't required by law to publish an article about their own wedding, Kingman," I pointed out. "Or release the pictures and video she shot."

"Well, I think there should be a law!" an irate voice sounded at our immediate rear.

We all whirled around, and found ourselves looking into the furious furry face of Shanille. Shanille is cat choir's conductor, but she's also Father Reilly's cat, and Father Reilly is the person who was supposed to marry Odelia, until she decided to cancel.

"Uh-oh," Harriet muttered next to me.

"Can you please explain to me why you decided to cancel that wedding?!" Shanille practically screamed.

"We didn't cancel anything, Shanille," I was quick to point out. "Odelia did all the canceling, and we were just along for the ride."

"But you were there! You should have said something! You can't just cancel a wedding! Father Reilly is so upset he's started drinking again!"

"Father Reilly has become an alcoholic?" I asked.

"Coffee, not alcohol. And he knows it's not good for him."

"I'm sure Odelia's wedding had nothing to do with that."

"It had everything to do with it! Father Reilly had the most beautiful wedding planned. It was going to be the highlight of his career. Never would there have been a more beautiful wedding. It was going to be a day people talked about for generations to come. And then—nothing! Not a word! Not a single peep from the Pooles!"

"Oh, poor man," said Dooley. "Maybe he should get married himself. That way he can enjoy the wedding of his dreams, and since he's the one getting married it won't get canceled."

"Unless the bride cancels," said Harriet.

"He first has to find a woman who wants to marry him," said Brutus.

"Catholic priests don't marry, you dimwits!" Shanille practically shouted.

"But why?" asked Dooley. "Don't they like getting married?"

"Don't try to cloud the issue," said Shanille, pointing a threatening paw in my friend's direction. "You should have convinced your human to let that wedding go through."

"You overestimate the influence we have on our human, Shanille," I said.

"Yeah, Odelia is a grown person who doesn't listen to us," Harriet argued.

I smiled at this, for I'd had this argument with Harriet before, and she'd taken the view that I should have stopped Odelia from flying to Vegas and antagonizing the whole town. Looked like now that Shanille argued the same thing Harriet had switched sides.

"You did it on purpose, didn't you?" said Shanille, wagging that threatening finger in Harriet's face now. "You know how excited I was about staging the cat choir performance to end all cat choir performances, and you willfully and purposely set out to sabotage my moment of glory. Admit it!"

"I admit no such thing!"

"You know what? I don't think I can tolerate this kind of behavior any longer, and so I don't think I will." She raised her head high and gave us that supercilious look she does so well, and regarded us from between narrowed eyes. "Consider yourselves expelled!"

"Expelled?" I asked. "Expelled from what?"

"Expelled from cat choir!" she said, then started to walk away, even before we had recovered from the shock, adding, "You're not welcome anymore, same way I wasn't welcome at your wedding!"

"But... it wasn't our wedding!" Harriet cried.

But her pleas fell on deaf ears, for Shanille had left the gathering.

———————

6

"*W*here do you think you're going?" asked Vesta when her friend opened the car door.

"I have to pee," said Scarlett. "Why? Do I need to ask permission?"

"Where are you going to pee? There's no bathrooms that I can see."

"There's a vacant lot over there behind that fence. That all right with you?"

Ever since they'd launched the neighborhood watch, Vesta had been thinking of a simple solution to a problem that had vexed them from the start: both she and Scarlett were ladies of a certain age, and their bladders weren't what they used to be, meaning that if they sat in a car all night, following doctor's orders in regard to the regular intake of fluids, there came a moment they needed a bathroom break. Unfortunately, Hampton Cove wasn't exactly littered with public restrooms, and since bars and restaurants were mostly closed by the time they started patrolling those mean streets of their small town... It was one of those vexing problems, and thus far they hadn't been able to solve it—apart from peeing in the bushes, of course.

"Or maybe I'll go to that house over there," said Scarlett now, as she pointed to a derelict structure right next to the empty lot. The house looked ripe for demolition.

"Better don't go in there," Vesta advised. "Place is a crack house."

"You think so?"

"Why do you think we're parked out in front of it?"

"I thought you wanted a quiet spot to eat our midnight snack."

Scarlett always brought a midnight snack, as both women got those midnight cravings most people get, but amplified by the fact that they were engaged in a high-peril endeavor, which as everyone knows makes the blood pump faster, which in turn makes you hungry. She wasn't sure this was all scientifically kosher, but it was her explanation for the phenomenon and damn if anyone said it wasn't so.

"My contact at the precinct tells me drugs are being dealt out of this here house," said Vesta. "And I want to catch them in the act, snap some pictures, and get them all arrested."

"Your contact at the station? You mean your son?"

"No, I don't mean my son," she scoffed. "If it were up to Alec we wouldn't even be out here patrolling. I'm talking about Chase. At least he's on our side. Unlike my own son, who seems to think we're just two crazy old ladies out to create trouble."

"Look, I don't care if that's a crack house," said Scarlett. "I need to use the bathroom, and if I wait much longer I'm going to have to go right here in your car."

"Maybe we should get you those Poise Pads. The heavy-duty ones."

"Hey! I'm not *that* old!"

"Okay, so go if you have to. But don't say I didn't warn you."

"Maybe you can come with me?" Scarlett suggested. "And bring the pepper spray," she added. "And the stun gun."

"I'll bring the stun gun, the pepper spray and my ex-husband's shotgun," said Vesta as she grabbed the gym bag that sat patiently on the backseat for just such a contingency. So far they hadn't seen a lot of action, but she had a feeling that was about to change.

So they both got out and Vesta suddenly got one of those bright ideas that sometimes came to her out of the blue. Probably as a consequence of all the vitamin B she'd started to pop. She'd read somewhere it helped boost your brain activity. "You know what?" she said. "We should probably pretend that we're two drug addicts looking to score. That way we can catch these drug dealers in the act!"

"Isn't that called entrapment or something?"

Neither of them was exactly on top of the finer points of the law, but that had never stopped them before. "Who cares? Don't you want to stop these people from selling drugs to kids?"

"I don't have any kids," Scarlett reminded her.

"I'm not talking about your kids. I'm talking about all the kids, Scarlett."

Scarlett rolled her eyes. "Honestly? I just want to pee."

Just then, the door to the crack house suddenly flew open, and a man came hurrying out. He was holding his phone and was talking into it, even as he crossed the street and got into a car, which just happened to be the car Vesta and Scarlett were parked right behind. In a reflex action Vesta snapped a picture of both the man and the car, and as it drove off, Scarlett suddenly yelled, "Fire!"

"I know, right?" said Vesta. "We're on fire tonight!"

"No, there's a fire!" said Scarlett, and pointed to the crack house.

"No shit," said Vesta as she saw that Scarlett was right: the house they'd singled out for their big drug bust was on fire—smoke wafting from the door the man had left ajar.

"We gotta do something!"

"It's probably those crack dealers," said Vesta. "They must have turned the heat up too much when they were cooking all of that crystal meth." She pressed the phone to her ear and bellowed, "Yeah, Dolores. Vesta Muffin. I want to report a fire at a crack house!"

"You got a fire in your crack?" asked the raspy-voiced dispatcher with a chuckle.

"Watch your tongue, Dolores. I'm being serious here."

"Well, that's a first," said the wise-cracking dispatcher.

She placed her hand over the phone and addressed her friend, who now stood pressing her legs together awkwardly in an attempt to hold her pee. "You better start putting out that fire while I try to explain to Dolores what's going on here."

"Put out that fire? I'm not a fire putter-outer kinda girl, Vesta."

Vesta crooked an eyebrow. "You need to pee, right? Well, better get started." And as Scarlett gave her an eyeroll, she grinned.

Just then, she saw the curtains move at one of the houses located directly across the street from the crack house. And as she watched, the face of a woman briefly appeared, then disappeared into the shadows again.

Looked like they weren't the only ones keeping an eye on things.

7

*I*n spite of the fact that Shanille had told us we weren't welcome anymore at cat choir, the four of us decided to defy her outrageous dictum and go anyway. After all, who was Shanille to decide we couldn't join the biggest social gathering in town?

Harriet, specifically, was outraged, as she kept referring to the whole thing as *Shanillegate*, though I wasn't exactly sure what she was talking about.

"What if she throws us out?" asked Dooley, who abhors physical violence of any kind.

"She can't throw us out," I said. "She would need the support of the entire cat choir and I'm sure they don't feel the same way Shanille does."

"But what if they do? What if all the cats in Hampton Cove hate us from now on?"

"I'm sure they don't," I assured my friend.

And so we decided to risk it, and set paw for the park that night. And I have to say that things weren't as harrowing an experience as I'd surmised. Frankly, I'd been bracing myself on our trek over, mentally countering all the arguments

Shanille might throw at us, and even testing the muscles in my right paw in case one of her lieutenants took a swing at me. Well, you know how it is. You build up this big thing in your head, and start arguing back and forth, putting words in the mouth of the party of the second part and then thinking up the best ways to cancel them out, and when it all comes down to it, the whole thing turns out to be one big nothing-burger and you wasted all that mental energy for nothing.

"Look, maybe I exaggerated a little when I told you that you weren't welcome anymore," said Shanille as she walked up to me. "But you have to admit you played a pretty dirty game, Max."

"But we didn't play any game at all!" I cried, all those arguments in my head coming to the fore all at once. "Odelia felt that the wedding was too much for her, and so she decided she was better off canceling the whole thing. We were never consulted, Shanille, believe me."

And even if we had been consulted, we would have heartily agreed with our human, as we personally had decided to skip the wedding, even though at a later stage Gran had arranged a safe spot for us, where we wouldn't be trampled underfoot by the masses.

"I wanted to come to the wedding," said Harriet. "Vesta had arranged with Father Reilly that we could sit out in front, right next to the altar. And I was really looking forward to having the place of honor, you know. To have a front-row seat to the thing."

To be perfectly honest Harriet hadn't been all that excited. Even seated out in front she'd been afraid someone was going to step on her precious tail and reduce it to mush, and frankly so had I.

Shanille stared at Harriet, her jaw having dropped a few inches. "Father Reilly did what?"

"He said we could sit out in front," Harriet repeated,

unaware of Shanille's consternation, or maybe extremely aware and eager to rub it in. "Next to the altar?"

"But that's *my* spot!" said Shanille. "I always sit out in front during Mass. Everybody knows that that spot is reserved for Father Reilly's cat, and *I'm* Father Reilly's cat. Not *you*," she added, pressing a paw into Harriet's chest. "*Me!*"

"Please take your paws off me," said Harriet, who's very particular when it comes to her precious fur being soiled by the paws of other cats—or human hands for that matter. Well, she has a point, of course. Who knows where those paws or hands have been, right?

"You're lying," said Shanille.

"No, I'm not. Vesta said we could sit right next to the altar."

"No, she didn't."

"Yes, she did!"

"No, she. Did. Not," said Shanille, accentuating every word with another jab in Harriet's chest.

Harriet pressed her lips together, and I could see that something was bubbling underneath the surface. Like a volcano, this particular cat was about to explode. I would have warned Shanille, but something told me she was beyond being reasoned with.

"If you touch me one more time…" Harriet began.

"Then what?"

"I will scratch you," said Harriet simply.

Shanille laughed a throaty laugh. "You'll do no such thing. I'm the leader of cat choir. If you scratch me, you're out for good."

"I swear to God, Shanille, you do not want to see me angry," said Harriet, in the tone she likes to adopt when she's about to skin a person alive and boil their remains.

"I'll do whatever I want," said Shanille, and gave my friend a shove that landed her on her tush.

"Oh, no, you didn't," said Harriet, and then, with a low growl, she hauled off and... actually gave Shanille's snoot a light tap!

"Hey!" said Shanille, looking stunned.

"I warned you. You do not put your filthy paws on me."

"Dooley," I said, "I think I just saw that stork."

"You did? Where?!" he said excitedly.

"Come, I'll show you," I told him curtly, and walked off with my friend. And even as we removed ourselves from the scene, I could hear the telltale sounds of a cat fight breaking out: the caterwauling, the screeching, and the fur being ripped to shreds.

"Poor Shanille," said Dooley. "She was really looking forward to that wedding, wasn't she?"

"Yeah, I guess she was," I said.

"So where's the stork?" he said happily as he glanced around, then up at the trees and the night sky above, regarding those twinkling stars and that full moon with an expectant look in his eyes.

"Well..." I said as we paused at a nearby tree and I gave it a pointed look. "This is just the darndest thing. I'm sure I saw it sitting in this very tree just moments ago."

"But... it's not there anymore, Max."

"No, I can see that. Why, shoot. Looks like we missed it."

"Oh, darn," said Dooley. "Now Odelia will have to wait a little longer for her firstborn."

"Yeah, I guess she will," I said. And as we walked on, I decided that cat choir was probably a bust, so we decided to head on home instead. And as we exited the park, and found ourselves out on the sidewalk, suddenly a familiar car drew to a stop at the curb, and the window rolled down.

"I caught a killer you guys!" Gran yelled from the car. "I caught my very first killer—all by my lonesome!"

"Not by your lonesome," Scarlett corrected her friend's rash statement. "I was right there with you, remember? We both caught him."

"You caught a killer, Gran?" asked Dooley, admiration dripping from his words. "How did you do that?"

"Well, we just happened to be parked outside a known crack house, and we were about to go in and make a bust when this guy comes out, looking suspicious."

"Very suspicious" Scarlett confirmed.

"He hopped into his car, and I managed to take a picture of the guy and the car." She glanced down at a little notebook she always keeps handy when she's on her nightly patrols. "Guy by the name of Joshua Curtis. Dolores looked up the license plate for me."

"Joshua Curtis!" said Dooley. "But that's Odelia's client!"

"Odelia's what?" asked Gran, much surprised.

"Odelia took on a client this morning," I explained. "Unofficially, of course. Something about an infidelity case he wanted her to check out."

Gran blinked and shared a look of consternation with her friend. "Well, looks like Odelia's client just went and killed three people."

8

When the calls came in Odelia and Chase were seated side by side on the couch, Netflixing a romcom and enjoying this time together in post-wedding bliss. She still wasn't completely used to the fact that she was now Mrs. Chase Kingsley, and that she was a married woman.

"Do you want another home-baked muffin, husband?" she asked.

"I would love one, wife," said Chase with a grin. "Though to be absolutely honest, if I eat another one I'll probably burst."

"Me too," Odelia admitted. "Though they did come out pretty great, husband."

"I know, right?"

She settled herself against Chase, and purred, "When I married you I didn't know I was marrying a baking prodigy... husband."

"Beginner's luck. I bet that when I try that second batch they'll probably come out horrible."

"Now, don't say that. Don't disabuse me of my sweet illusions that the man I married could, any time he wanted to, start a career as a baker."

"Do you want to be married to a baker?"

"Nah, I love the fact that you're a cop."

And that's when the phone rang—both their phones. Chase's correspondent was Odelia's Uncle Alec, and her own was her grandmother, who sounded a little breathless.

"Odelia!" she practically yelled into the phone, causing the latter's offended ear to give a little lurch. "I'm so sorry, honey. If I'd known he was your client, I'd have kept my mouth shut, I swear!"

"What are you talking about?"

"The guy—your client—Joshua Curtis. How was I supposed to know!"

She sat up a little straighter. "What happened?"

"He came running out of that crack house that was on fire, acting all suspicious, so naturally I took a picture of the guy, and his car, and I sent it to Dolores. And now they're on the lookout for him. Turns out he killed three people!"

"What?!" she cried, jerking up with a start.

It wasn't long before she and Chase were out of their cozy jammies and into their regular street clothes and hurrying out the door.

"Triple homicide?" asked Chase as he slammed the car door shut and so did Odelia.

She nodded. "Turns out the guy they want for the murders is my so-called client."

"The one who wanted to stop his best friend's wife from having an affair?"

"Yup," she said. "Better step on it."

"I fully intend to," he said, and did indeed do as he'd promised. They made record time and within ten minutes were parking across the street from the place that Joshua

Curtis allegedly had tried to burn down to the ground—three people still inside.

The fire department was present, rolling up their hoses, and the street was a regular beehive of activity, firemen walking in and out of the building, as well as police officers.

Inside, they quickly met up with Odelia's uncle, who looked a little sleepy, as if the phone call had roused him from a deep slumber. Charlene Butterwick was also there. As the mayor of Hampton Cove it was probably her duty to be present at these tragic events. She, too, looked a little sleepy, and an image flashed through Odelia's mind of Uncle Alec and Charlene having been in the same position as Odelia and Chase just before, with both of them having fallen asleep next to one another on the couch.

"So what happened?" asked Chase.

"Three squatters, all of them dead. Two badly burned—pretty much beyond recognition, one died from smoke inhalation in the next room, but still recognizable." Uncle Alec raised his eyebrows meaningfully. "You'll never guess who it is."

"Just tell us," said Odelia. She wasn't in the mood for guessing games, to be honest.

"Franklin Harrison."

"The son of Herbert Harrison?" said Chase. "The real estate king?"

"One and the same."

"Wasn't he in some kind of trouble?" asked Odelia.

"You can say that again. Picked up several times the last couple of months. Some DWI, minor drug charges, contempt of cop..."

"So what was the son of one of the richest men in Hampton Cove doing in a squat?" asked Chase.

"Beats me. Maybe he was trying to score some drugs? This place has a bad reputation in that department."

"Gran tells me you've got a suspect?" said Odelia, deciding not to mention that said suspect was sort of a client of hers.

"Yeah. Probably the first time that neighborhood watch of hers does something right. Guy by the name of Joshua Curtis was seen exiting the premises shortly before midnight. He hurried to his car, talking into his phone, then took off like a bat out of hell."

"Here to score a fix, you think?" asked Chase.

"Possibly. Though from what I know of him he's as straight-laced as they come. Clerks at a notary public's office. One of those guys who would tell on his grandmother if he caught her jaywalking."

"Clean record?" asked Chase.

"As clean as a whistle. But we're still going to pick him up for questioning." He checked his watch. "In fact the officers I sent are on their way to lift him off his bed as we speak." He shrugged. "At the very least he's a witness, and if we're lucky, we got our guy."

Odelia excused herself. She'd just seen a little red Peugeot drive up, and knew exactly who was behind the wheel. She flagged down the car, and even before it had fully come to a standstill, she was already jerking open the rear passenger door and getting in.

"Step on it," she said. "We have to beat the cops."

"Oh, goodie," said Gran, and stomped down on the accelerator.

Scarlett grinned. "We're seeing more action in a single night than all of last month!"

"Odelia?" said Dooley, who she discovered was seated next to her, along with Max. "We missed the stork. Max saw him, but by the time we got there, he was gone."

She patted his head distractedly. "That's all right, Dooley. I'm sure I'll live."

9

*O*delia was clearly in a big hurry, and it took us some little time before she revealed to us why this was, exactly.

"Joshua Curtis is about to be picked up for questioning," she revealed, looking tense, "and before that happens I want to talk to him first. Find out what's going on."

"It's not very nice of Joshua to murder those people," said Dooley. "He shouldn't have done that."

"I'm not so sure he did do that, Dooley."

"You think he's innocent?" I asked, interested in this novel theory.

"I don't know. But I intend to find out before he's locked up in my uncle's slammer."

It didn't take us long to arrive at our destination, and judging from the light that was blazing in the window the man was still up. Which just goes to show: not all killers are the stone-cold kind, and some do get rattled when they've just murdered three people in cold blood.

We all got out of the car, and hurried up the drive. Odelia applied her finger to the buzzer, and when the door was yanked open, and Joshua Curtis appeared, he looked as tense as Odelia did. "Miss Poole!" he exclaimed. "I didn't expect to see you here." He then stared at Gran and Scarlett, clearly expecting an explanation, which Odelia declined to supply.

"The cops are on their way to pick you up," she said, "so you better start talking, Joshua. What were you doing on Parker Street tonight?"

"Oh," said the man, his face falling.

"Three men are dead, Joshua. And the police think you had something to do with it."

He gaped at her. "Me!"

"You were seen leaving the scene of the crime. In fact you were walking out of the house just as smoke started to appear. What do you have to say for yourself? And better talk quick. Like I said, the police will be here any second now."

He grimaced, as if her words didn't come as a great surprise to him. "Look, I wasn't—I had nothing to do with whatever happened there. I just… happened to pass by that place when I suddenly saw smoke coming out. So I did what any decent citizen would: I checked if there was a fire, and when I saw that there was, I immediately called 911."

"*You* called 911?"

"Of course. It's my civic duty to inform the emergency services whenever I become aware of an emergency in progress," he said, sounding very much like the law-abiding citizen and stickler for upholding the law he appeared to be.

Odelia seemed much sobered by this, and more at ease than she was when she'd hurried over there lickety-split. "So… what were you doing out there, exactly? It's not your neck of the woods now is it?"

"I… I was walking my dog," he said, and unfortunately didn't sound very truthful as he said it.

"I didn't see no dog," Gran said, putting in her two cents.

"I didn't see no dog either," Scarlett confirmed.

"These two ladies saw you," Odelia explained.

He blinked, then said, "My dog must have been back in the car by the time they saw me. His... his paws get cold."

Now there are people who are very adept at lying, and then there are others who are not so adept. And Joshua Curtis belonged in the last category, I'm afraid.

"His paws get cold," said Odelia, sounding skeptical.

"He's very sensitive. He gets cold paws."

"Do you even have a dog, sonny boy?" asked Gran, narrowing her eyes.

"Of course I do. Boomer!" he called out. "Boomer, come here, boy." He listened for a moment, then shrugged. "He's probably asleep. Boomer is very old," he added as if entrusting us with a confidence.

"Look, I hope for your sake, Joshua," said Odelia, "that your story is true. Because the police..." She paused as the sound of a police siren could be heard, piercing the nocturnal silence that descends over most small towns the moment night falls.

"Here they are now," she announced. She wagged a finger in her client's face. "Better tell them the truth, Joshua. No lies, you hear me?"

He smiled. "I'll tell them exactly the same thing I just told you."

"He's lying, Max," Dooley said as we returned to the car, just as a police car pulled up to the curb and two officers got out.

"Yeah, I had that same impression," I said.

"I mean, if he had a dog, it was the unsmelliest dog that I've ever not smelled."

"You didn't smell a dog?" asked Odelia.

"Nope," Dooley confirmed. "The man doesn't own a dog and has never owned a dog. If he had, we would have smelled him, wouldn't we, Max?"

"Absolutely."

"What are they saying?" asked Scarlett, as usual tickled pink by our chattering.

"They're saying they smelled a rat," Gran grunted.

"A rat!"

"Not a real one. The guy is lying through his teeth. He doesn't have a dog."

"So if he wasn't walking his dog, then what was he doing out there?"

"Scoring dope? Murdering three people in their beds? Who knows?"

"Oh, dear," said Odelia as we all got back into Gran's little car. Across the street two officers had now entered Joshua's house. "Gran?"

"Yah."

"Are you sure you didn't see a dog?"

"She doubts us, Max," Dooley whispered.

"A good detective always double-checks," I whispered back.

"Nah. Not a dog in sight."

"Darn it."

"Look, I'm sorry, honey," said Gran. "If I'd known he was your client, I wouldn't have gabbed."

"It's not your fault, Gran. It's Joshua's fault that he got himself into a world of trouble. Can you bear with me for just five more minutes?"

And with these words, she got out of the car again, and hurried across the street.

"What's she up to now?" asked Gran.

"Trying to get her client off the hook?" Scarlett suggested.

"He's not really her client," I said. "He's just a guy who asked her to do a thing."

But the finer nuances were lost on Gran, as she intently watched her granddaughter engage one of the officers in conversation. "Gee, he's for it now," she suddenly said. And as I looked where she was pointing, I saw that the other officer was escorting Joshua out of the house, equipped with a shiny pair of handcuffs.

"Looks like Boomer isn't just an old dog," said Scarlett. "He's an invisible one, too."

And as one officer deposited Joshua into the squad car, Odelia came jogging back and let herself fall into the seat next to us with a deep sigh. "They've got something on Joshua but they won't say what it is. Clearly his story about walking his dog and just happening to be in the vicinity of that house is nonsense."

"Of course it is," said Gran. "I thought we'd established that already."

"So what was he doing there?" asked Scarlett. "And why is he lying about it?"

"Beats me," said Odelia.

"It's not nice when clients lie to you," Dooley said. "They should always be telling you the truth because you're the best friend they have when they're in a pickle."

In spite of her irritation at her lying client, Odelia smiled, and so did Gran. "You're absolutely right, Dooley. Now why don't you tell Joshua Curtis that?"

"Do you think I should? Can he understand what I'm saying?"

"No, honey, I don't think he can," said Odelia.

"Pity," said Dooley. "I could have made him talk." To which we all laughed heartily—except Scarlett, of course. Though after Gran translated Dooley's words, she laughed even harder than the rest of us.

"You know what you should do?" said Gran at length.

Odelia was frowning before her. "No, what?"

"You should prove that your client is innocent."

"He's not my client, Gran. He's just a guy who asked me to do him a favor."

"Well, then you should prove that your not-client is innocent."

"I don't know if he's innocent, do I?"

"So prove that your not-client is not not-innocent!"

When Odelia groaned, Scarlett patted her hand. "I know how you feel, honey. I have to put with this every. Single. Night."

"Oh, shut up," Gran grumbled, starting up the car. "You love it."

"Yeah, I do," said Scarlett with a grin.

And then we were off again, trying to prove... something.

10

*T*he next morning Dooley and I were on the road again, this time in the wake of our human, who was ready to tackle this thing the way it should be tackled: with fortitude and a quizzical mind. So following our example, she decided to drop by the General Store. Though in all honesty I don't know if picking Wilbur Vickery's brain was such a good idea—Wilbur's brain being not all that interesting to pick. Though the man does have a fount of gossip to spread about our local populace, of course.

And so while Odelia was shopping for wares and gossip, we sat down with Kingman, who looked a little nervous when he caught sight of us. I soon learned it wasn't us he was nervous about but the twosome who stepped up behind us: Harriet and Brutus.

"H-hi there," said Kingman as he eyed Harriet a little trepidatiously. "H-how are you this fine morning, your highness?"

"Your highness?" said Dooley. "I didn't know Harriet was royalty, Max?"

"She's not," I said. "It's just a way of showing respect for a person."

"A sign of deep, deep, very deep respect," said Kingman with a congenial smile. "Deep respect for a person I deeply… respect. Isn't that true, Harriet?"

"Well, I'm sure I'm honored," said Harriet, who seemed different this morning. I don't know exactly in what sense, but she definitely was. For one thing, she had this supercilious smile on her face that seemed stuck there with super-glue, and nothing appeared capable of fazing her, which isn't like the Harriet I know. Also, even after the fracas of last night, there wasn't a scratch on her. Not a single bit of fur out of place.

"So Odelia's client was arrested last night," I said, wanting to get this show on the road. "You don't happen to know anything about the guy, do you Kingman?" I asked.

"His name is Joshua Curtis," Dooley supplied helpfully.

"Um… no," said Kingman. "Can't say that I do." He was still eyeing Harriet with a slight sense of alarm that I found very peculiar.

"No gossip that you know of?" I insisted. I couldn't imagine that Kingman would be totally unaware of Mr. Curtis's particulars, as he's usually so well-informed.

"I'm telling you, Max, I don't know anything about this guy. Not a thing. He's a nobody. A complete zero. Never done anything, never been on anybody's radar until now."

"He killed three people," Dooley said. "So he's probably on everybody's radar."

"We don't know that he killed them," I said. "It's quite possible that he's completely innocent, and that he has a good explanation for what he was doing there."

Just then, Shanille came walking up. Contrary to Harriet, she did look a little… damaged. More than a few patches of fur were missing from her corpus, and there was a thick scratch right across her nose.

"Shanille!" said Dooley. "What happened to you?"

Shanille directed a scathing look at Harriet. "*That* happened to me. Your *friend*."

Harriet's look of smug satisfaction deepened. "Oh, you're not still sore about our little tiff, are you, Shanille?"

"Tiff? Have you seen me? I look like I've been in the wars! Even Father Reilly was worried. He wants to take me to the vet, if you please! Figures I've been attacked!"

"You should consider that a good thing," said Harriet. "It shows that he cares."

I was starting to understand now why Kingman was treating Harriet with such deference. He probably had witnessed the massacre, and didn't want to be next on Harriet's list.

"Look, if you insult my human," said Harriet, "you should know that I won't take it lying down. So as I see it, you got exactly what you deserved. Isn't that right, Brutus?"

"Yup," said Brutus. He cut a look in my direction, and I could tell that he wasn't fully committed to Harriet's tough new stance, taken straight from The Equalizer's playbook.

"Well, you're still out," said Shanille. "No more cat choir for you."

"I don't think so," said Harriet.

"You're out of cat choir, I'm telling you."

"Nope. I'm still very much in."

"I'm the director and I'm telling you that you're suspended until further notice. And if it were up to me—"

"But it's not up to you, is it, sweetheart? You can't just kick out a cat without a majority of cat choir endorsing your position. So why don't we put it to a vote?" She approached Shanille, who moved back a step. "Why don't we ask the members of cat choir if they feel their star soprano should be sidelined, just because the director says so, mh?"

"Harriet, I don't know if…" Brutus started to say, but she shut him up with a single glance.

"I will win this thing," she said. "I'm popular. Cats *like* me. They *love* me. They *adore* me. And I will win this vote with a smashing majority. Just you wait and see."

"I'll vote for you, Harriet," said Kingman obsequiously.

"I know you will, Kingman," said Harriet, batting her eyelashes at the stocky cat. "Now are we done? What are you guys doing here, anyway?"

"Odelia's not-client didn't murder three people last night and now she's not trying to prove that her not-client is not not-innocent," said Dooley, then frowned. "Or was it the other way around?"

"I think we should probably see what's taking Odelia so long," I said, feeling that soon Harriet would start canvassing us for our support. And frankly? Even though Harriet is my friend, and I mostly enjoy her company, I wasn't sure I could condone this use of physical violence to settle her arguments.

So we moved into the store, and clearly just in time, for we found our human cornered by no less than three members of the public. Reading from left to right, they were Father Reilly, Wilbur Vickery and Ida Baumgartner.

11

"*W*hat you did isn't Christian, Odelia, dear," Father Reilly said. "Getting married in Las Vegas?" He shivered visibly. "That den of iniquity? That bastion of sin? You should have gotten married right here, standing before your own community, in the church where you were baptized, the church where your parents were married, and your grandmother—though of course that was before my time." The thought of Gran seemed to pain him a bit, so he cleared his throat and said, "What do you have to say about this, Wilbur?"

"Well, I agree with you wholeheartedly, of course, Francis. Getting married in Vegas is simply not done. Not by a nice girl like Odelia, anyway."

"Or by a God-fearing police officer like Chase Kingsley," Ida Baumgartner added.

"Look, I'm truly sorry things happened the way they did," said Odelia, "but—"

"No buts," said Father Reilly. "All is not lost, Odelia. I say we regroup and reschedule. Your wedding may be postponed but it's not canceled. I consulted my planner this morning and I can fit you in for the second weekend of February. How does that sound?"

"That sounds absolutely wonderful," said Ida, who was one of Odelia's dad's most faithful and regular patients. In fact she never skipped a week without paying the good doctor a visit and always had some new symptoms to reveal. "Thank you so much for your understanding, Father," she continued. "And for giving Odelia this second chance."

"Look, I think it's very kind of you to do this," said Odelia, "but—"

"Could we maybe reschedule, Francis?" asked Wilbur, who'd been consulting his diary on his phone. "The second weekend of February is a little difficult for me. I've got something going on. The national coaster collectors convention in... Vegas, of all places," he added with an awkward little laugh. "But the weekend after I'm free."

"That would be... the third weekend of February," said Father Reilly, taking out his own phone. "I could slot you in. But it would have to be the Saturday. On Sunday I have a wine tasting I can't be late for in the early afternoon. It's all the way in... well, Vegas."

Ida, who was consulting her diary, shook her head. "Can't. Third weekend of February is completely full. The next available weekend is... May. First weekend in May."

"No, I'm afraid I'm fully booked that weekend," said Father Reilly. "Another wine tasting," he added curtly.

Max, who'd joined the revels, now pshh'ed, and said, "Better skedaddle while they're not looking!" And Odelia smiled and decided to follow his advice. So she left Father Reilly, Wilbur and Ida to find a date for her wedding, without having the courtesy to consult her, and decided Max was right. Time to go! As it was, they didn't even notice that the bride, supposedly the star of the wedding, was no longer amongst those present.

"I'm so glad I decided to do the wedding in Vegas," she said as she hurried out of the shop. "The more I think about it, Max, the more I'm starting to see that these people aren't interested in me or my wedding. All they want is an opportunity to have a party—at my expense!"

"Well, you don't have to worry about that anymore," said Max. "The wedding is done, and there won't be a reprise."

"Father Reilly seems to think there will be a reprise."

"Just avoid him for a while. He'll get the message," advised her cat.

"You know, Max, you're a lot wiser than most humans I know, and that includes the three I just left in there."

"Dooley, watch out!" said Max suddenly.

Dooley, who'd been walking with his head up, staring at the sky, almost bumped into a lamppost.

"Dooley, you have to look where you step," said Odelia as she picked up the small gray cat, who was still inspecting the sky, even though he'd almost bumped his snoot into an unyielding object.

"I have to watch for the stork, Odelia," he said. "If I don't watch for the stork, how will he know where to find us? And then he won't be able to deliver your babies."

"Oh, so now it's more than one baby already, is it?" she said with a grin at Max.

"I'm not sure," Dooley admitted. "How many did you order?"

"Well, to be completely honest with you, I didn't order any babies, Dooley."

"No babies! But you have to put in your order, Odelia, otherwise how is the stork going to know what you want?"

She laughed heartily and hugged the small cat close. He was such a sweetheart.

But then they'd arrived at the police station, and it was time for more serious business: she'd decided that she wanted to visit Joshua and have another chat with him. If he really was innocent, he had to stop lying and start telling the truth.

So she dropped Dooley to the ground and walked in.

*D*ooley and I both felt sorry for Odelia. It isn't every day that your human is cornered by the parish priest and two of his most fervent parishioners and pretty much bullied into organizing a wedding for the entire town.

"I hope Odelia doesn't go through with it," I said therefore.

"But she has to have the babies, Max," said Dooley. "She just has to."

"I wasn't talking about babies, Dooley," I said. "I was referring to the wedding Father Reilly is so desperate to organize. Besides, why are you so anxious for our human to have babies anyway? She's still young. She has plenty of time to start a family."

"But if she doesn't have babies now she will kick us out!"

"How so? I don't get it."

"Okay, so Shanille told me that women should get pregnant on their wedding night. That means that they're blessed. If they don't get pregnant on their wedding night, it means that something is wrong with the marriage, as the man cannot... perform?"

I had to suppress a smile at this. "I don't think you should listen to Shanille, Dooley. Her world views aren't always, um, an accurate depiction of reality, let's put it like that."

"But if Odelia doesn't have babies immediately, she'll be upset with Chase, and she'll get divorced. That's what Shanille said. If the husband can't perform, the woman has every right to ask for a divorce, because the only purpose of marriage is to have babies, and plenty of them."

"Okay, so let's get this straight. According to Shanille, if Odelia doesn't have babies immediately, she should file for divorce, as it's a sign that Chase isn't the right guy for her?"

"That's what Shanille said. And she told me to look out for that stork. If I miss it, and those babies get delivered to the wrong address, Odelia will kick Chase out and get a divorce! And then she'll be sad, and she might kick us out, too! Because we like Chase so much," he added quietly.

"Look, Dooley, this is all just a lot of baloney. Please don't listen to Shanille. If she tells you a lot of stuff that doesn't make sense, you ask me first before you go start believing her, okay?"

"So… was she lying, Max? Was Shanille lying when she told me that Chase needs to perform or else? And what does she mean by that?"

"Um…"

"I asked her if she meant that Chase had to sing for Odelia. You know, perform a song? Or maybe a dance? And she looked at me and shook her head and walked off. So now I still don't know what she meant."

"Well, you called it, Dooley," I said. "When a couple gets married the husband has to perform a song and a dance. And if they do it right, they'll make their brides very happy."

Dooley smiled. "I'm sure that Chase did a great job. I've heard him sing and he's aces."

Chase is a wonderful human being, a great cop, and an amazing partner to our human, but what he is not is a singer. In fact Chase can't sing if his life depended on it. And I've never seen him dance, but somehow I don't think he's aces in that department either. But if Dooley was happy to think that he was, good for him. I wasn't going to rob him of that particular illusion.

"You keep watching out for that stork, Dooley," I said therefore. "But if it doesn't arrive soon, I don't want you to worry, all right? Stork or no stork, Odelia loves Chase, and I'm sure that he loves her, too. So there is no danger of divorce in their near future."

"That's good to know, Max," my friend said earnestly, "cause Shanille really had me worried there for a minute."

And since Odelia was such a wonderful human, we decided to give her a helping paw by spying on Uncle Alec, who, for some reason I couldn't quite fathom, didn't seem as eager as usual to share information with his favorite niece.

So we rounded the building, hopped up onto the Chief's windowsill, and lay in wait, making sure we weren't seen, and pressing our ears to the window to pick up those telling clues Odelia likes us to supply her with.

"So it was definitely murder?" we heard Uncle Alec ask Chase.

"Yeah, no doubt about it," said Chase. "And we know who did it, too, which is a first."

"Joshua Curtis. Notary clerk. No priors, not even a speeding ticket. In every respect a model citizen. And now this."

"The toxicology report is clear: all three of these guys died from smoke inhalation, and all three had Rohypnol in their blood, which proves they were knocked out prior to their deaths."

"So they were knocked out first, then someone set fire to the building?"

"Exactly. So now we know what happened, and we got the killer. Only thing we don't know is why. Why did Mr. Model Citizen suddenly bust loose and decide to slay three?"

---

*O*delia, in spite of the fact that she wasn't the man's attorney, and she wasn't a police officer either, still was granted access to Joshua Curtis. She'd told the desk sergeant that the man was her client, and no further questions were asked. Such was the advantage of being the Chief's niece that five minutes later she was sitting in one of the interview rooms talking to the suspect.

Joshua looked a little worse for wear, compared to the last time she'd seen him: his shirt was untucked and his chin was dark with a shadow of stubble. He also looked a little sleepy, and clearly hadn't enjoyed his short sojourn in the pen.

"So are you finally going to tell me the truth, Joshua?" she said.

"What do you mean?" he asked, warily dragging a hand through his tousled hair.

"You weren't walking your dog last night, were you? You don't even have a dog. So what were you doing at the house on Parker Street?"

He hung his head in resignation. "Look, all I wanted to do was have it out with the guy once and for all, all right?"

"What guy?" asked Odelia with a frown. "What are you talking about?"

"The guy! The guy Melanie was seeing."

"But… I thought you said you didn't know who he was?"

"I… well, I may not have told you the complete truth," he admitted. "His name is Franklin Harrison, and apparently he was living in that squat house for some time. Even though he hadn't told Melanie. He'd told her he was living in Jackson Heights."

"The luxury condos?"

He nodded. "He lived at Jackson Heights for a while, but he was kicked out by the home owner's association. Complaints about the use of intoxicants and all-night parties and scantily clad girls in the corridors. Oh, and he didn't pay the rent. That probably had something to do with it as well. Anyway, when I found out Melanie was seeing this Harrison guy, I asked around, and discovered he'd moved to the squat house, probably having a good time shacking up with his fellow drug addicts." He shook his head in disgust. "Not the kind of guy Melanie should be involved with. And I'm pretty sure she didn't even know all there was to know about him. Like the drugging and the squatting."

"I don't get it," said Odelia. "He's Herbert Harrison's son, right? So he must be loaded. So why didn't he pay the rent on his condo? What was he doing living in a squat house?"

"Beats me," said Joshua. "All I know is that when you told me yesterday that he'd dumped Melanie I was relieved, but not so relieved as not to want to make sure he never got near Melanie ever again. So I decided to pay him a visit and tell him exactly that. Only when I got there I saw that the place was on fire, and Harrison's lifeless body lying on some ratty mattress, looking very much dead." He raised tired eyes to meet Odelia's. "Look, I didn't kill him, all right? I didn't set that building on fire, whatever the police are saying. I was just in the wrong place at the wrong time, that's all. My rotten luck for wanting to help Jason save his marriage."

"But if you're innocent, why did you run off like that? Why didn't you stick around?"

"Because I didn't want to get involved. I don't want Melanie to know I was sticking my nose into her personal business, and Jason even less so. If Melanie knew I'd been talking to her boyfriend, or asking you to look into this whole messed-up business, she would probably never talk to me again, and neither would Jason." He sighed and hung his head. "I really messed up big time, didn't I?"

"You should have told me, Joshua. you should have told me you knew who Melanie was seeing."

"I know, I know." He looked up. "Can you help me? You're the Chief's niece. And the lead detective is your husband. You must have some pull with these people. Can't you explain to them that I'm innocent?"

She placed a hand on his arm. "Are you sure you told me everything this time?"

"Yes, of course."

"No more lies?"

"No more lies."

"I'll talk to my uncle. Find out what he knows. The fact that they're holding you here means they must have something on you. Though it could be just like you said: being in the wrong place at the wrong time." She fixed him with a stern look. "But you'll have to come clean, Joshua. You're going to have to tell them everything—every last detail."

"Also about Melanie?"

"Also about Melanie."

"Oh, God," he said, and rubbed his haggard features. "She'll be so angry with me."

"Well, that can't be helped," she said. "If you don't want to be charged with triple homicide you're going to have to come clean, and that means telling my uncle and my husband exactly what you just told me."

"All right, if you say so. What a mess."

"You can say that again."

14

"*D*ooley, keep your head down!" I whispered when Dooley raised his head to look through the Chief's window.

Lately Uncle Alec had expressed his resentment with us cats spying on him. He didn't seem to enjoy the experience as much as I'd thought he would. In my view only people who are trying to hide something resent being spied upon, so what was he hiding?

At any rate, it probably behooved us to keep our noses down.

"So all three victims had Rohypnol in their systems?" the Chief was asking.

"Yep. All three of them were knocked out with the same drug. And what's interesting is that we found the exact glass used in the process."

"But with only two sets of fingerprints," said Uncle Alec. "The killer's, and one of the victims."

"Yeah, that's the strange thing. Though it's possible the killer used different glasses to accomplish his purpose. At any rate, we've got Joshua Curtis's fingerprints on the glass with the remnants of the drug, and Franklin Harrison's prints on that same glass, which proves that Joshua was the one who handed Harrison that drink, and knocked him out. We couldn't lift Harrison's prints from the body, as his hands were too badly burned, but we had his prints on file."

"No doubt it's Franklin Harrison?"

"No doubt. His relatives have already identified him."

"So what about motive?"

"Now listen to this, Chief," said Chase, clearly very happy with himself. "It's a doozy. So Franklin Harrison was having an affair, okay? We found plenty of pictures of one Melanie Myers on his phone, and flirty texts back and forth. Real hot stuff, okay?"

"Uh-huh."

"So get this. This guy Joshua Curtis is Melanie's husband's best buddy. And not just that, the guy's been in love with Melanie for years and years and years. I mean, to the point of obsession, okay? I'm talking pictures and videos of the woman on his phone."

"Of Melanie Myers?"

"Sure! The guy's phone is like a private throne on which he worships the woman's likeness. And what's more, the two of them used to be an item, before the husband entered the picture. We know this because we found a diary at the guy's office, hidden at the bottom of his desk drawer, where he talks about the affair, and about his feelings for her. Turns out they briefly dated in college, before she fell for his best friend."

"Jason Myers," the Chief supplied.

"Exactly."

"And the guy never stopped carrying a torch for the woman."

"Looks like he's in love with her to this day, Chief. And

I'm sure that once we go through his house with a fine-tooth comb we'll find plenty more to corroborate this."

"So what's your theory?"

Chase took a deep breath. "Okay, so my theory is that Curtis found out that Melanie was cheating on her husband with Harrison and got mad, then decided to get even. So he devised a plan to make sure Harrison never crossed paths with Melanie ever again."

"And what about the two other victims?"

"Pretty sure they weren't the intended target, Chief. What I think happened was that he figured that if he killed all three of them we'd think we were dealing with a serial killer, when in fact his intended target was Harrison all along."

"He must have seen too many movies."

"Exactly. Only that's the problem, isn't it: Joshua Curtis isn't a crafty killer. He made so many mistakes that we got to him even before the bodies of his victims were cold. He left the glass with his fingerprints and the Rohypnol at the scene. He set the room on fire by dousing it in gasoline, probably hoping to make it look like an accident but failing miserably, and he was seen by two witnesses exiting the place and getting into his car."

"Look, one thing, Chase," said Uncle Alec. "You know that this Joshua character asked Odelia to follow Melanie around, right? Supposedly to figure out if she was having an affair and who with."

"Yeah, I know. She told me."

"Well, I'm not sure she isn't still in the guy's corner, so to speak."

"But surely if she learns the truth…"

"That's exactly it. I don't think it's a good idea to involve her this time."

"What do you mean?"

"I mean that I have the impression she's willing to go to

bat for the guy. She's in here right now, you know talking to him."

"She is?"

"That was Dolores on the phone just now, telling me your wife is talking to Joshua Curtis, and probably being told by the guy that he's innocent, and asking her to try and prove it."

"You don't think…"

"Yes, I do." He let drop a pregnant pause. "I think we can't afford to let Odelia know what we know, since she'll probably tell Curtis, and he'll use it to stage a defense. So from now on, not a word about this case to your wife, you got that? At least as long as she's willing to go to bat for the killer."

"You mean…

"As much as it pains me to say this, we're obviously working on opposite sides of this thing, Chase. Your wife is working for the suspect—against us!"

Just then, Dooley popped his head up again, and I could hear Uncle Alec utter a curse word, and when I glanced up surreptitiously, I found myself looking into the Chief's eyes, his face so close to mine on the other side of the window, I was momentarily startled. But then I smiled and gave him a little wave. Futile, of course. First of all because humans can't discern those subtle expressions we display, so he probably missed my smile by a mile. And my conciliatory little wave? That only seemed to solidify his utter annoyance.

"Will you stop spying on me!" he yelled, a clear indication he wasn't happy with us.

"Yes, Uncle Alec!" I yelled back.

But of course he couldn't understand me.

15

"I thought I'd find you here," said Chase when he came upon Odelia, who was patiently waiting in his office.

Odelia was in Chase's swivel chair, and had taken the time to think about her recent interview with Joshua Curtis. Somehow she still had the feeling that he hadn't told her everything, though why he would lie to her she did not know. Unless, of course...

"Do you think he did it?" she asked her husband.

Chase took a seat in front of his own desk and gave his wife a look of appraisal. "You know that your uncle has forbidden me from discussing this particular case with you?"

"He has? But why?"

Chase shrugged. "He seems to think we're on opposite sides. You're in the killer's corner and we're in the victim's."

"So you think Joshua is guilty."

"Guilty as hell," Chase confirmed.

"So you must have proof, right? To back up that claim?"

"Sure we have proof. But like I said, I'm not allowed to discuss it with you, since the Chief is afraid you'll just turn around and supply that information to Curtis, helping him stage his defense."

"I would never do that," said Odelia, shaking her head. "If he's guilty, that is."

"Well, it sure looks like he's the one that did it, babe."

"But why? What makes you so sure?"

Chase heaved a deep sigh. It was probably bad for him to deny his wife the kind of information that would help her crack this case, knowing she was probably as excellent and determined a detective as he was. "Look, if I tell you, you have to promise me not to tell your uncle, all right? Cause if you do, I'm in deep doo-doo."

"Scout's honor," she said, holding up two fingers.

"And I don't need to remind you not to tell the suspect anything we're about to discuss."

"Absolutely. Frankly I have a feeling he hasn't been entirely honest with me. Even though he says he's told me everything, I still feel he's holding out."

"You bet he is. Did he tell you that he and Melanie Myers used to be an item?"

"No, he did not."

"They weren't together long, but the guy is still carrying a torch for the woman."

"That, I noticed. Though I thought he was mostly looking out for his friend."

"I doubt that. I think he was jealous, and couldn't stand that Melanie was seeing Harrison. So he killed him and tried to make it look like an accident by setting fire to the place."

"How did Harrison end up a squatter?"

"Well, turns out that Franklin Harrison has a brother named Marvin, and from what I understand Franklin was the bad boy and Marvin the responsible one. Franklin was always the rich kid with the gazillions of friends, partying all the time, and getting into all kinds of trouble, while Marvin's main focus was the family business."

"Real estate, right?"

Chase nodded. "Commercial and industrial real estate, mainly. Herbert set up the company and turned it into a goldmine, and hoped his sons would take an interest. Only Franklin decided he was too busy spending daddy's money to bother with the business."

"And dating married women," Odelia added.

"Exactly."

"So while Marvin minds the family store, his brother is living it up."

"Only at some point Daddy must have had enough, and decided to cut him off. So Franklin found himself without funds, and living as a squatter in the dump he died in."

"And what about those two other guys?"

"Took us some time to identify them. They were both badly burned." He glanced down at his little notebook. "Aldo Kali and Tomio Iberia. Both well known in connection to multiple drug-related incidents. Been arrested multiple times the last couple of years."

"Drug dealers."

"Looks like Joshua set fire to the room those two guys were sleeping in, with Franklin in the next room, which is why they were burnt to a crisp, and Franklin only suffered minor burns, though there's still extensive damage to his lower limbs and his arms."

"But you think Franklin was the intended target."

"Absolutely. You should have seen what we found on Joshua's phone. Pictures of Melanie, videos of Melanie, and in his office a diary completely devoted to Melanie."

Odelia processed all of this. "I don't know, Chase. I just don't see him as a cold-blooded killer. You've seen him. You've talked to him. He's as straight-laced as they come."

"Those are often the worst offenders, babe. You know that as well as I do."

"But killing three people, just because one of them was having an affair with the woman he's been in love with for years? If that's true, then why didn't he kill Jason Myers?"

"Because Jason is his best friend. And even though he probably hates the fact that Melanie ended up with Jason, he more or less got over it. And then along comes this spoiled rich kid Harrison and starts something with his precious Melanie—his dream girl. I think he got so angry he wasn't thinking straight. And Harrison just had to die."

She smiled at her husband. "Looks like we're working the case together again, only this time my uncle isn't supposed to know."

"Yeah, and better keep it that way. He's been getting all kinds of flack about the wedding, and he's not in a good mood right now."

"What do you mean, flack?"

"Oh, just the usual, you know," said Chase, a little evasively.

Just then, the door opened and one of Chase's colleagues stuck her head in. It was Sarah Flunk, one of the officers, and when she saw Odelia she said, "Oh, there she is. Miss Grinch who stole our wedding." And shaking her head, she closed the door again.

Chase and Odelia shared a look of understanding. "I think I see what you mean," she said dryly.

16

ince Uncle Alec clearly didn't want us to spy on him, we decided to try a different tack: we snuck back into the precinct and decided to spy on Dolores instead. Dolores Peltz is at the heart of the police station, as the station dispatcher and desk sergeant she knows everything there is to know about what goes on in that place. So it was with great expectations that we took a seat next to her desk, and settled in for the duration.

We didn't have to wait long, for soon after we arrived a woman and a man walked into the station, claiming to be one of the victims' mother and brother.

"I want to see the person in charge," said the woman. She was the matronly type, and clearly used to getting what she wanted. Her hair was done up into a sort of tower of hair, and she wore plenty of makeup. Her son was the clean-cut business type, with a nice suit, tortoiseshell glasses perched on his nose, and sandy hair that had all the hallmarks of having been arranged by a very expensive hairdresser. Not Fido Siniawski, in other words.

"And you are…" said Dolores in her raspy smoker's voice.

"Franklin Harrison's mother," said the woman. "And this is my son Marvin."

"Could you please take a seat in the waiting area?" said Dolores. "I'll get someone to come and talk to you right away."

Mother and son removed themselves from the scene, and soon we were surprised by the arrival of Odelia, our very own human.

"Dolores," she said, "who are those people?"

"The Harrisons," the dispatcher said. "Mother and son. Here to see the manager." She flashed Odelia a little grin.

"I want to run something by you," said Odelia.

"Sure, go ahead. Though I have to tell you that I'm probably one of the only people in this town still willing to talk to you right now."

"How so?" asked Odelia, looking surprised.

"The wedding, silly girl! You can't dangle a big carrot like that in front of people's noses and then yank it away again at a moment's notice."

"I'm sorry. But we simply couldn't go through with it."

"Oh, you don't have to explain to me," said Dolores, waving an airy hand. "I understand perfectly. If my wedding had ballooned to such ridiculous proportions I wouldn't have wanted to go through with it either." She gave Odelia a reassuring smile. "Don't you worry about a thing, sweetie. People have a very short memory. Just you wait and see. This time next week they'll have forgotten all about it."

"I hope so," said Odelia. "Father Reilly wants me to do the wedding the first weekend of February, Wilbur Vickery the second weekend, and Ida Baumgartner in May. The three of them pulled their diaries and are trying to fix a date. They didn't ask me for my opinion, so they clearly don't need me to be there. Probably just to pull my checkbook."

Dolores laughed. "I can just imagine their faces when they found out the wedding was canceled! They must have been so annoyed!"

"Anyway, so I wanted to ask you about last night's fire."

"Uh-huh. Shoot."

"So you got the call, right?"

"I got three calls, in fact."

"Three calls?"

"Sure. Just lemme check." She tapped a few keys on her computer. "Here we go. So the first call came in at eleven forty-eight, okay?"

"Who made the call?"

"I don't know. They didn't give me a name. Said they wanted to report a fire on Parker Street. Then the second caller didn't give me his name either. This was at eleven fifty. And then a minute later your grandmother called in."

"Okay."

Dolores took off her reading glasses. "So the second caller sounded kinda winded, as if he was walking and talking. And of course we now know that the second caller was Curtis, as he was calling from his own phone, the dumbass." When Odelia gave her a look, she added, "You have to be pretty dumb to call in your own crime from your own phone, Odelia!"

"Unless he didn't do it."

"Yeah, right. So the only thing that struck me as odd is that the Dibbles didn't call in."

"The Dibbles? Who are they?"

"Bart and Vanda Dibble. They're neighbors. They live right across the street. They're usually the first to call when something happens at Parker Street 51. In fact they've called in so many times I've considered blocking their number."

"You wouldn't do that, right?"

"Nah, I'm not allowed. Unfortunately."

"What do they usually call about, these Dibbles?"

"Oh, the usual, you know. Noise complaints. Parties happening late at night, drug dealing, and of course the fact that the building was the home of a bunch of squatters, which they said was bringing down property prices and the value of their own home."

"They're probably right."

"Oh, sure. But they don't have to call and tell me about it every single day, do they? Besides, it's not as if I can help it that the owner of the building has decided to let it get run down like that. We informed the town council, and they promised to look into it."

"Looks like the Dibbles finally got what they wanted," said Odelia. "That building will probably have to be demolished now." She gave the other woman a quick hug. "Thanks so much, Dolores. You're the best."

"Yeah, yeah, yeah. Go on, get out of here." She then glanced down at Dooley and myself. "And you too, Humpty and Dumpty. Get lost. I don't need a couple of cat spies on my ass all day."

And as we walked off, I said, "She spotted us, Dooley. I didn't think she'd spot us."

"Why did she call us Humpty and Dumpty, Max?" asked Dooley as we left the precinct in Odelia's wake.

"We really need to work on our stealth mode. I can't believe she saw us."

"So who are you, Max? Humpty or Dumpty?"

"I dunno," I muttered, still wondering how Dolores had spotted us. I prided myself in the way I could surreptitiously spy on people, only now I'd been found out two times in a row: first by Uncle Alec, though that was entirely Dooley's fault, of course, and once by Dolores, and in this last case I had nobody to blame but myself.

"I think I'm Humpty, Max," said Dooley. "And you're Dumpty."

"Sure, Dooley," I said. "Whatever you say, buddy."

17

*O*delia and her two feline detectives had arrived at the place where Melanie Myers lived with her husband. She'd first tried to find her at work, at wefindyourdreamhomeforyou.com, but one of her colleagues said that Melanie had called in sick. Odelia hoped she wasn't too sick to talk to her, though.

The house was a nice modest family home with a single garage in a neighborhood of similar family homes. It was one of those neighborhoods where not too many cars drive through, and where kids can take their bikes out and play on the street. Two little boys were doing that in front of the Myers house, and Odelia wondered if they were Melanie's. Joshua hadn't mentioned any kids, but then Joshua hadn't exactly been forthcoming.

She walked up to the house and pressed her finger on the buzzer. A pleasant jangling sound echoed inside, and before long she heard footsteps and the door was opened.

"Yes?" said Melanie Myers, looking a lot plainer than she'd looked the day before. Gone was the makeup, and gone was the nice suit she'd worn—probably office attire. She was plainly dressed in jeans and a T-shirt now, and her hair was done up into a messy bun.

"Melanie Myers?" asked Odelia.

"Yes, who's asking?"

"My name is Odelia Poole, and a friend of yours asked me to help him out with something. Joshua Curtis? I believe you know him?"

"Yes, I know Joshua," said Melanie.

"Can I come in for a moment? It's a delicate matter."

Melanie considered this, then glanced down and caught sight of Max and Dooley, or Humpty and Dumpty as they now called themselves. "Oh, how cute!" Melanie exclaimed, immediately crouching down and tickling both cats under their chins. The purring sounds made it obvious they weren't averse to her ministrations. "Are they yours?"

"Yeah. Yeah, they are. They like to follow me around, as strange as that may sound."

"Oh, no, mine are just the same," said Melanie. "If I'd let them they'd follow me to the office and lie next to my desk all day. Unfortunately my boss hates cats. She thinks it's unprofessional and makes a bad impression on the clients." She rolled expressive eyes. "As if cats could ever make a bad impression on anyone. I'd say they're an ice breaker."

Well, they'd certainly broken the ice now, Odelia thought as she stepped inside the house and closed the door behind her.

Two cats came walking up to her, meowing all the while. They were very small, even smaller than Dooley, and were clearly purebreds. So she left Dooley and Max to deal with them, and maybe extract some more information, and followed Melanie into the living room.

"Please take a seat," said Melanie, indicating a beige leather couch on which crocheted covers had been placed to protect the leather against the sharp claws of her fur babies.

"I don't know if you've heard," she said, "but Franklin Harrison was found dead last night."

Melanie was shocked by this piece of news, Odelia could tell, but she tried to hide it well. "I-I'm afraid the name doesn't ring a bell," she said unconvincingly.

Odelia decided to put all of her cards on the table. Joshua might not like it, but that couldn't be helped. "Joshua told me that you and Franklin were seeing each other," she said therefore. "So he asked me to find out if this was true. He wanted you to stop, as he was afraid of the impact the affair might have on your marriage, so…"

"Oh, God," said Melanie, shifting in her place. "Joshua told you that?"

"He did. Yesterday morning. He asked me to follow you around and take pictures."

"Pictures!"

"Yeah. He wanted to confront you with the affair, and make you stop."

Melanie shook her head in utter dismay. "I don't know how he found out. But then Joshua likes to stick his nose where it doesn't belong," she said with a touch of vehemence.

"The thing is the police have arrested him. They think that he killed Franklin."

Melanie sat up straight. "Joshua killed Franklin!"

"He says he didn't do it. He says he just wanted to talk to him, but when he arrived the house was on fire and Franklin was dead."

"How-how did he die?" asked Melanie.

"Smoke inhalation. But before that he was drugged. So he didn't suffer."

Melanie lowered her gaze to the floor. "I did have an affair with Franklin," she said in a low voice. "But it didn't mean much. Not to me, and not to him either. In fact he called me yesterday to break it off. Said the relationship had run its course and he didn't think we should see each other anymore." She shrugged. "It was clear from the beginning that this wasn't going anywhere. It was just a fling for him—and for me, too, I guess."

"How did you meet?"

"At a club. I don't usually go clubbing anymore. Not since I married and had kids."

"Oh, so those two boys outside…"

Melanie smiled. "Yeah, they're mine. My precious little darlings." She looked up at Odelia. "Are you married, Miss Poole?"

"Just got married, actually," said Odelia, displaying her wedding ring.

"When you've been married as long as I have, you'll understand that from time to time a woman needs to have a night out—some little time off from her marriage, especially when there are kids involved. Don't get me wrong, I love my husband, and I adore my two rascals, but we have this thing where I take one night off every month, and so does Jason—that's my husband. So I have a girls night, and he has a boys night—not on the same night, obviously—and it makes you forget for just one night that you're not just a mom and a wife but also a woman, you know. I go to the spa with my girlfriends, or we hit the town, or take a weekend off and go someplace to be pampered and have fun. So last month we went clubbing, which I hadn't done in years, and it was such a blast."

"And you met Franklin."

"Yeah, he's one of those people who never stop clubbing. He hit it pretty hard that night, but I'd probably had a little too much to drink, and I was having such a good time, and so we danced a little, and talked some, and when all was said and done and he offered to share a cab, I said yes, and we ended up kissing in the backseat. And when he invited me over to his place I said yes, which probably I shouldn't have done." She sighed, and twisted her wedding ring. "Franklin is one of those people who's a lot of fun to be around, you know. A real playboy, in the literal sense of the word. He's just fun, fun, fun, and, well…" She shrugged. "I guess I needed a bit of fun just then. Jason and I have been going through a rough patch, and Franklin was my escape. I'm not proud of what I did, and I hope you won't tell my husband, Miss Poole. He'll be devastated."

"I won't tell him, but Joshua might," said Odelia, not wanting to give the woman any illusions.

"Yeah, Joshua is a dear friend, but he's also a meddler."

"Is it true that you and he used to be…"

"Oh, God! Did he tell you that? No, we were never a thing. We went out on one date in college. One single date, and we shared one kiss. That's it. The next day I met Jason and it's just been him ever since." She smiled a weak smile. "Still is, actually, no matter what you may think."

"I think you should probably tell your husband about your affair," said Odelia, "before he hears it from someone else. Or before your kids hear about it. You know how quickly gossip spreads in this town."

"I know," said Melanie. "Thanks for letting me know." She glanced in the direction of Max and Dooley and her own two cats. "And thanks for bringing your babes along on a play date. They seem to have hit it off together."

18

*W*hile Odelia was busy talking to Melanie Myers, Dooley and I got busy interviewing her cats. Well, I say interviewing, but what happened was more of a monologue... by those cats.

"Oh, my God you guys are so scruffy," said one cat, whose name, if I had heard her right, was Musti.

"So, so scruffy," her friend echoed. She went by the name Susi.

"Who does your grooming?" asked Musti.

"Yeah, you guys have got *the* worst groomer."

"We don't have a groomer," I said.

They stared at us, then at each other, then back at us. "No groomer?" asked Susi.

"Well, that explains things," said Musti.

"We groom ourselves," said Dooley proudly.

More shared looks of astonishment. "Self-grooming? No way."

"Yes, way," I confirmed. "We groom ourselves. In fact most cats I know groom themselves."

"But... that's just horrible," said Susi.

"That's terrible," said Musti.

"Don't tell me you guys still use your..." Susi quickly stuck out her tongue, causing her friend to shiver with sheer disgust.

"Yep, that's how we do it," I said. "The good old-fashioned tongue."

"No way!" said Musti. Or maybe it was Susi. They were hard to distinguish.

"That's so disgusting!"

"No wonder you look so scruffy."

"So terribly scruffy."

And at this point they seemed to feel that they'd shared the same space with two scruffy self-groomers long enough, for they quickly tripped up the stairs and out of sight. Though as they went, we could clearly hear their conversation.

"Can you believe that Melanie would allow those two disgusting creatures to enter our house, Susi?"

"Now she'll have to sanitize the whole place, Musti."

"Sanitize? You mean sterilize."

Dooley turned to me. "I don't think they like us, Max."

"No, I think you're right, Dooley. They don't like us very much."

"We're not that dirty, though, are we, Max?"

"We're not dirty at all, Dooley. In fact I think we're perfectly nice and clean."

"Now we don't get to ask them questions."

"Somehow I have the impression that wouldn't have made much difference." Musti and Susi didn't strike me as the kind of cats we'd been able to extract a lot of crucial information from.

At least with those two out of the way we were free to take our measure of the house, and when we entered the kitchen we soon came upon a regular cornucopia of cat food.

And since Musti and Susi had commented on our lack of hygiene, but hadn't strictly forbidden us from dipping into their food supply, we decided to strengthen the inner cat and ate to our heart's content.

When we walked out of the kitchen, we saw that Odelia's interview was at an end, but just as we walked out, the front door opened and Melanie's husband walked in. At least I think he was her husband, since she kissed him and called him sweetie.

"This is Miss Poole, sweetie," said Melanie, making the necessary introductions. "She's here to ask us about Joshua."

"Joshua?" said the guy, who was short and sort of chunky. "What happened?"

"He's been arrested, I'm afraid, Mr. Myers," said Odelia.

"Arrested!"

"For murder," Melanie supplied.

Mr. Myers seemed absolutely agog by these revelations, which made me assume that Joshua hadn't yet been in touch to give him the news about his recent escapades. They might be best friends, but this was the kind of thing Joshua clearly didn't feel compelled to break to his friend any time soon.

"Can I ask you a couple of questions, Mr. Myers?" asked Odelia.

Melanie didn't seem excited by the prospect of our human talking to her husband, but complied nevertheless. "I'll go and check on the boys, shall I?" she said, and removed herself from the scene after a quick worried glance at her husband.

"The thing is, Mr. Myers," said Odelia, "Joshua came into my office yesterday—I'm a reporter for the Hampton Cove Gazette, by the way, but I also consult with the police and do some detective work from time to time." She hesitated.

"He probably wanted you to follow Melanie around, is that it?" asked Mr. Myers.

"He's clairvoyant, Max!" said Dooley.

"Yes, he did," said Odelia, as surprised as we were.

Mr. Myers smoothed his shirt and settled down on the leather sofa. "I haven't discussed this with my wife, but I know she was having an affair. I don't know who with, and frankly I don't care." He glanced through the window, which looked out onto the street. We could see two kids playing on their bikes, their mother now watching over them with a keen eye and chatting with one of the neighbors by the looks of it. "My wife and I have been married for fifteen years, and don't get me wrong, we love each other very much. It's just that, from time to time Melanie feels the need to... bust loose, shall we say? To feel young again, with no responsibilities, no mortgage and no kids to take care of. And you know what? I let her. I know it doesn't mean anything. I know it's just a way for her to blow off some steam before she comes home to me and the boys again. And she always does."

"That's very..."

"Yeah, I know it's a little weird, maybe, but that's just the way it is. From the moment we started dating we decided to give each other space."

"And do you enjoy the same, um... privileges?"

"I do, as a matter of fact," said Mr. Myers with a curt laugh, "but I don't use them. I've never cheated on my wife, Miss Poole, and I don't think I ever will. And in all the years we've been together I can count on the fingers of a single hand the number of times Melanie's been unfaithful to me." He shrugged. "So I try not to let it bother me too much."

"So when Joshua tried to keep this a secret from you—"

"He shouldn't have bothered, because I already knew. Joshua is a good friend, but I think I know my wife better than he does. I trust her, and apparently Joshua doesn't, if he feels the need to ask you to follow her around." He seemed a little annoyed by the initiative of his best friend, I thought.

"Do you think Joshua is capable of murder?"

"Joshua? A murderer? Absolutely not. He couldn't kill a fly."

"He seems to have feelings for Melanie," said Odelia.

"Oh, yeah, I know he does. He loves her to bits. They briefly dated in college, you know. It didn't mean anything."

"It may not have meant anything to your wife, but apparently it meant a lot for your fiend, Mr. Myers," Odelia pointed out. "And now the police seem to think it was the reason he killed three people last night."

"Three people?"

"According to the police his intended target would have been Franklin Harrison."

"Name seems to ring a bell," said Mr. Myers, nodding.

"Franklin Harrison was the man your wife was having an affair with."

He blinked. "Okay."

"So now the police think that Joshua wanted to get rid of him once and for all."

Mr. Myers scooted forward and fixed Odelia with a serious look. "Do you believe he's guilty, Miss Poole?"

"Honestly? I'm not sure."

"Well, I am. Joshua didn't do it. No way in hell is that man capable of murdering three people in cold blood."

"Even if he thought he was doing it to save his best friend's marriage?"

Mr. Myers sat back again, and shook his head. "It all seems a little extreme."

"Just a routine question, if I may, but where were you last night, Mr. Myers? Around midnight, let's say?"

He produced a weak smile. "Are you accusing me of going after my wife's lover now?"

"Not at all. Just dotting the I's and crossing the T's."

"Well, I was here all night, and so was my wife, by the

way. We watched a movie and then went to bed. By the time I turned off the lights it was after midnight."

"Can anyone confirm that?"

He glanced out at his two boys. "I can vouch for my wife, and she can vouch for me. Isn't that enough?"

19

*V*esta still felt a little guilty about the role she'd played in the capture of Joshua Curtis, her granddaughter's client.

"It just isn't right, Scarlett," she told her friend as the twosome rode in her daughter's little red Peugeot Vesta liked to use. "If Odelia represents this guy that means he's innocent. I know my granddaughter. She would never defend a killer. And if only I'd known he was her client, I'd never have told my son about him. No way."

"You would have let that building burn to the ground?" asked Scarlett, who clearly wasn't fully on board with this mission yet.

"Oh, I would have called 911 for sure," said Vesta, "but I wouldn't have mentioned seeing Joshua."

They were on their way to Joshua's house right now, since Vesta felt they'd gotten the guy into the soup, and now it was up to them to get him out again.

"Look, I don't feel good about this, Vesta," said Scarlett, "I'll be honest with you. If we get caught…"

"If we get caught I'll just tell those cops that we're working under Odelia's instructions."

"But we're not!"

"Technically, maybe, but in the spirit of the thing we're fighting on her side."

"What side? The guy is obviously guilty. You saw him come out of that building."

"Just because the man came out of the building doesn't mean he's a killer," Vesta insisted. "He could have just been there to, well…"

"To do what? Pay a house call? I didn't even know notary clerks made house calls. But even they do, they damn well don't make them in the middle of the night."

"Look, I'll admit that I don't know what the guy was doing there. But I'm sure he had a good reason, and I'm sure in due course he'll tell Odelia, who'll tell us, and then I'll prove to you that what we're doing is right and just and— holy crap will you look at that?"

She was referring to the pileup that involved no less than two police cars and three regular cars. The police cars still had their lights a-flashing, but clearly that hadn't done them any good.

"Probably on their way to Joshua Curtis's house," said Scarlett.

"Then we better make sure we get there first," said Vesta, and stomped the accelerator practically through the floor of the aged car.

Moments later they arrived in a cul-de-sac and parked in front of a nice little house with a neat little front yard. It even had a select smattering of garden gnomes livening things up, something which would have pleased Vesta's son-in-law to no end.

"Let's do this," she announced as she got out of the car.

"How are we going to get in?" asked Scarlett as she

tiptoed up to the house, as if afraid someone might hear her. As usual, she was dressed in a tight miniskirt and crop top, her high heels making it a little hard for her to remain inconspicuous, as did her choice of clothes. Vesta, on the other hand, was dressed for the job: a gray tracksuit with yellow trim, and sneakers.

"I got a set of master keys," said Vesta, as she held up the set proudly.

When Scarlett looked a little closer, she frowned and said, "That's not a master key set. That's a set of lock picks."

"It was called a master key set on eBay, so that's what it is." She picked a small sharp instrument from the collection and inserted it into the keyhole. It looked like something a surgeon would use to poke a hole in a person. "There was an instruction manual included," she explained as she inserted a second sharp instrument and started jiggling.

"Who was the seller? Burglars, Inc?"

"Probably," said Vesta as she stuck her tongue out and jiggled away to her heart's content. "The trick is in the jiggling," she explained. "If you jiggle long enough, something has to give."

Unfortunately nobody had relayed this information to the lock, which remained unwilling to play ball.

"Maybe we'll have a look around the back," she said after a while. "Before the neighbors file a report."

So they moved around the house and found themselves in an equally neat backyard with a small porch and Vesta repeated the trick with the instruments. Finally, when she didn't have more luck than at the front door, Scarlett said, annoyed, "Just let me try. Jiggling comes naturally to me." But instead of taking advantage of Vesta's master key set, she put her shoulder against the door, her hand on the handle, and gave it a hard push. Something budged, and suddenly the door swung open.

"How the hell did you do that?!" asked Vesta.

"You just need the right approach," said Scarlett.

"That door is probably male," said Vesta as both women pushed inside.

The house itself was as clean and neat as the outside had promised, and as Vesta took the ground floor, Scarlett moved up the stairs to check around.

"What are we looking for, exactly?" she asked as she walked off.

"Anything incriminating!" Vesta yelled after her.

"And then what?"

"Then we remove it and give it to Odelia. She'll know what to do."

"This is such a bad idea," Scarlett muttered, but did as she was told and hurried up the stairs.

Vesta checked the kitchen, which was so neat it could have served as a model kitchen at a kitchen trade fair, and opened a couple of cupboards. For the occasion she'd put on plastic gloves, and for a few moments she admired the kitchen, then decided to snap a couple of pictures. She'd been trying to convince her daughter to remodel the kitchen for a while now, and this was just the kind of kitchen Vesta thought would be perfect.

She then moved into the garage, flicked on the light and looked around. Near the door, she saw four yellow metal jerrycans standing neatly in a row.

"Huh," she said, and picked them up. "Empty," she murmured, then shrugged, and carried them to the door to take out to the car. When you're accused of arson it probably doesn't look good to have four empty jerrycans in your garage, she figured.

"Vesta!" Scarlett suddenly yelled. "You gotta see this!"

Vesta stomped up the stairs, afraid there would be more dead bodies. Even she couldn't explain away more dead bodies—or drag them to her car. But when she arrived upstairs, and followed Scarlett's voice into what looked like the master bedroom, she saw to her elation that there was no dead body on the bed—or anywhere else, for that matter.

"What?" she said, panting from the exertion of running up those stairs.

"Will you look at that?"

"Who's the babe?" asked Vesta as she took in the scene. A life-size painting of a nude hung over the bed, depicting some blond babe, her naked body draped across a sofa.

"Some movie star, you think?" asked Scarlett.

"Dunno," said Vesta, but got her phone out again and started taking pictures.

"Weird," Scarlett said as she shook her head.

"What's weird about it? Some guys like to stare at pictures of Babe Ruth, this guy likes to look at naked women."

"Woman—singular. I'll bet it's someone he knows."

"And I'll bet it's just something he picked up in a dime store. Anything else?"

"I haven't finished yet."

"God, you're slow."

"Oh? And what have you found, Miss Amateur Burglar?"

Suddenly a police siren could be heard, and both women shut up. Their eyes met.

"Let's skedaddle," said Vesta.

"Good idea," Scarlett agreed.

And so they skedaddled. And not a minute too soon, for even as Scarlett pulled the back door shut, they could hear the sound of a key being inserted in the front door.

"Damn fool," Vesta said as she and Scarlett hurried round, both carrying two jerrycans. They took a peek to see if the coast was clear. "Why did he have to give them the key?"

"Probably because he was arrested and forced to empty out his pockets?"

"You're such a smart-ass, did you know that?" said Vesta as they hurried to the car.

"I know. That's why you love me, right?"

"I do, sweetie," said Vesta. "No one else would be crazy enough to do this."

"Oh, so now you admit this was a crazy idea, huh?"

"Less talk, more skedaddling," Vesta grunted, and shoved down the accelerator. A cop glanced back as they drove past, and held up her hand for them to pull over. But too late.

We were back at Odelia's office, with Dooley and myself lounging in one corner, Harriet and Brutus in another, and Odelia herself busy typing on her computer. She was probably working out where to go from here. She's resourceful that way.

"So you still haven't told me if you're Humpty or Dumpty, Max," Dooley said.

Brutus guffawed. "Humpty Dumpty? What are you talking about, Dooley?"

"Dolores over at the precinct called us Humpty and Dumpty, but she didn't say who's Dumpty and who's Humpty and it's driving me crazy," Dooley confessed.

"I think you probably misunderstood," said Brutus. "I think she was referring to you as Numpty and to Max as Dumpty, for obvious reasons."

Harriet gave him a shove. "Brutus, don't be mean," she said.

"I'm not being mean. I'm just pointing out the facts."

"You're being a bully, and I don't like it," said Harriet. "So stop it already."

"Yes, Harriet," Brutus muttered as he placed his chin on his paws.

"So I'm Numpty and you're Dumpty?" asked Dooley.

I just shook my head.

Suddenly Gran and Scarlett came bursting into the office, carrying what looked like four jerrycans. "Look what we found!" said Vesta with a note of triumph in her voice.

"Jerrycans?" asked Odelia, showing us she's very perceptive.

"Bingo!" said Gran. "And guess where we found them!"

"Um... at the gas station?" said Harriet, putting her two cents in.

"At Joshua Curtis's place," said Scarlett.

Odelia shot up from behind her desk so fast I thought she must have had a rocket explode under her buttocks to lend her that much speed. "WHAT?!" she said.

"We went over there just now," said Scarlett, "to remove any incriminating evidence." She shrugged. "Don't look at me. It wasn't my idea."

"You did WHAT?!" Odelia said as she took three big steps and joined her grandmother and her friend.

"He's your client, Odelia!" said Gran. "We have to protect him against my son's unhealthy obsession with the guy. If he's your client, he's innocent, you can see how that's just basic logic, right?"

"But Gran!" said Odelia, as she took in the four jerrycans now dumped at her feet. "You found these at Joshua's house?"

"In his garage," said Gran. "They're empty," she added helpfully.

"I suggest you bring them to the police station at once," said Odelia.

"Are you crazy? We can't do that! It's exactly this kind of evidence that's going to make them convict the guy faster than you can say 'He didn't do it!'"

"We're not in the business of concealing evidence, Gran. We're in the business of finding out the truth."

"Even if it means a jury of his peers will have a hard time not convicting him of murder?"

"Even if it means that, yes."

"Told you," Scarlett said. "Show her what we found in the guy's bedroom."

Gran took out her phone and showed something to Odelia I couldn't see.

"Can you show us, too?" I asked therefore, and Gran happily complied. I think she would have shown these pictures to anyone, except her son maybe.

The pictures showed a very large painting of a very naked... Melanie Myers!

"Is that Mrs. Myers?" asked Dooley.

"Yeah, looks like," I said.

"But... why isn't she wearing any clothes?"

"Um, she was probably taking a bath," I said.

He craned his neck to take another look. "So where's the bath? All I see is a couch."

"Um..."

"So who is she?" asked Scarlett. "Some movie star? Singer?"

"The wife of his best friend," said Odelia, looking much sobered.

"The *wife* of his *best friend?!*" said Gran, and shared a meaningful look with Scarlett.

"See? Told you he was weird," said Scarlett.

"Okay, so clearly the guy is head over heels in love with the woman," said Gran. "But that still doesn't mean he killed anyone!" she hastened to add.

Odelia furrowed her brow as she thought this through. "So he had four empty jerrycans of..." She took a sniff from one of the jerrycans. "... gasoline in his garage. And a nude painting of Melanie Myers hanging in his bedroom." She heaved a deep sigh. "It's getting harder and harder for me to convince myself he didn't do it, you guys."

"Yeah, looks that way to me, too," I said.

"At any rate, you have to give these to the police. You can't keep them."

"I have no intention of keeping them," said Gran. "These are for you!"

"Well, I don't want them."

"We can't give them to the cops now. They'll want to know why we took them."

"How did you get in, by the way?"

"With my master key set."

"Lock picking set," Scarlett said.

"Master key set!"

"What a mess," Odelia said, dragging her fingers through her blond mane.

"We could always put them back," Scarlett suggested.

"And get caught? I don't think so," said her friend.

"Look, just come clean," said Odelia. "Uncle Alec won't be happy, but he won't be too upset either. After all, you can always say…"

"Yes?"

"Well, you could say…"

"Uh-huh?"

Odelia threw up her hands. "I have no idea what you could say, but I do know you can't keep these."

"Like I said, I wasn't planning on keeping them. They're yours."

"Oh, God."

"The guy's your client! You should keep them!"

"I'm not keeping those jerrycans, Gran. That's evidence in a crime. And not just any evidence, either. This is crucial evidence!"

"Well, duh. Why do you think I took it, dummy?"

"Gran is in big trouble now, isn't she?" said Dooley.

"No more than usual," I told him.

"So just tell us honestly," said Scarlett. "Do you really believe this Joshua Curtis guy is innocent?"

Odelia shrugged. "Right now I'm not sure what to believe. I'm just trying to get a clearer picture of what's going on here. And hopefully in the process find the truth."

"You know who could have done it?" said Gran, wagging her finger at no one in particular. "Those neighbors."

"What neighbors?" asked Odelia.

"The neighbors! We saw them peeking through the window, didn't we, Scarlett? And then pretending like they hadn't seen us."

"I talked to Dolores today," said Odelia thoughtfully, "and she mentioned that the neighbors have been launching a regular avalanche of complaints the last couple of months."

"See!" said Gran. "I knew I was onto something!"

"Even a broken clock gets it right twice a day," Brutus muttered.

"I heard that!" Gran shouted.

21

"That tip about the neighbors was a good one, I have to give her that," said Odelia as she steered her aged pickup through Hampton Cove, on her way to Parker Street.

"Like Brutus said, though," Max intimated, "even a broken clock gets it right twice a day."

"Yeah, but Dolores said much the same thing: the Dibbles really wanted those people gone. Is it too much to imagine that they might have gone to extreme lengths to get what they wanted?"

"I guess we'll soon find out," said Max, and she threw him a grateful smile through the rearview mirror.

Dooley and Max were in the backseat, as usual, while Brutus and Harriet had opted to head on home. They weren't in a sleuthing mood, apparently, and Harriet had said something about a showdown at cat choir she needed to get mentally prepared for, whatever that meant.

Odelia parked her car across the road from the derelict structure, now deserted and festooned with crime scene tape, and glanced up at the house where the Dibbles lived, husband and wife. She saw the curtain move, then drop back into place. "At least they're home," she told her cats, who were following in her wake.

"Now let's get them to talk," said Max.

"So if I'm Numpty, and you're Dumpty," said Dooley as they walked up to the house, "then who is Humpty?"

"I'm sure I don't know, Dooley," said Max, sounding a little weary.

"Could it be," said Dooley, "and this is just a theory, mind you. But could it be that Humpty is the name of the stork?"

"No, Dooley," said Max, "Humpty is not the name of the stork."

"How do you know? Have you ever met the stork?"

Odelia smiled as Max had to admit that Dooley had him stumped.

She pressed her finger against the mother-of-pearl bell button and listened to the loud buzz of the bell as it sounded inside. Moments later the door was opened a crack and two suspicious eyes studied her carefully. "Yes?"

"Hi, my name is Odelia Poole and I'm investigating last night's murder. The murder that happened just across the street? You didn't happen to see anything?"

"I already talked to the cops," said the woman, for now that the door was opened a little wider Odelia could see that it was indeed a woman. She would have pegged her in her late sixties, with a florid face and a hard expression in her eyes. Not a woman to be trifled with.

"I know, but I'm just working a different angle."

"Do you have a badge? The policewoman who was here last night had a badge."

"No, I do not have a badge," she said, "but if you want to check my credentials you can always get in touch with this person." She handed Mrs. Dibble Chase's card. "He's the detective investigating the case and I'm sure he'll vouch for me."

"Mh," the woman said, clearly not impressed. "So what do you wanna know?"

"Well, did you see anything suspicious last night? People entering the building or exiting?"

"I saw one guy exiting the building. Nice-looking fella. Looked like a lawyer. Not the kind of person you'd expect in a place like that."

"And what kind of place is that?"

"A crack house," the woman spat. "Filled with junkies and slackers. I've been complaining to the cops for months, but do you think they even showed me the courtesy to come and talk to me? No way. But now that three people are dead suddenly they all show up and start asking a million questions. If you people had listened to me sooner, this would never have happened!"

"I know," said Odelia. "So apart from the clean-cut type, did you see anyone else?"

"No one," said the woman, shaking her head. "Of course it's not as if I spent all night looking at that wretched place. I've got better things to do, me, and so does my husband."

"Can I talk to your husband, perhaps? Maybe he saw something?"

"He didn't see nothing."

"But—"

"Nothing!"

"Just one more question, Mrs. Dibble. Did you happen to call the police last night? Or your husband?" she hastened to add when the woman started shaking her head.

"I did not," said Vanda Dibble.

"Well, someone called the police."

"Two old ladies were out here, staking out the place. They called the cops."

"I know, but one more call was placed. Or actually two. The clean-cut individual, as you so aptly described him, called 911 and so did the two old ladies, but there was a third 911 call, and I was wondering…"

"Well, it wasn't us. Now if there's nothing else…" She started to close the door. Then suddenly there was a loud scream that came from somewhere inside the house.

"Vanda!" a man's voice called out. "I got 'em! Busted them fair and square!"

The woman quickly turned back to join her husband, and Odelia decided it behooved her to enter the house and see what was going on in there.

And as she followed Mrs. Dibble into the living room, then through to the kitchen and out into the backyard, she was met with a fascinating scene: there stood an old man, with a face as florid as his wife's and eyes as hard her hers, brandishing a gun at two old ladies. And those two ladies were… Gran and Scarlett!

"What are you doing here?" Odelia blurted out.

"You know these two?" asked Mrs. Dibble, whirling around.

"I caught them with these," said Mr. Dibble, and pointed to four empty jerrycans, lying at Gran's feet. "They tried to sneak into the tool shed, if you please!"

"You told me to get rid of them!" Gran cried. "So I figured what better place to dump them than here with these two killers!"

"I told you to take them to the police!" said Odelia.

"How do you know each other?" Mrs. Dibble tried again.

"I was gonna call the cops as soon as we planted them in the shed," Gran explained.

"I told you this was a bad idea," Scarlett hissed.

"It was a good idea. Only I hadn't counted on the old coot with the gun," Gran hissed back.

"Hey, who are you calling an old coot!" said the guy.

"You, you old coot," Gran snapped. "Just admit it, you killed those people! You set fire to that building across the street, didn't you? Confess!"

"Oh, just call the cops already, Bart," said Mrs. Dibble. "These two are obviously nuts."

"She's my grandmother," Odelia now explained. "So maybe you shouldn't call the police?"

"I thought you *were* the police!" said the woman, suspicion making her face flush.

"She's not a cop," said Gran. "She's a reporter."

"A reporter!"

"And a civilian consultant," Odelia added weakly.

"That does it. I'm calling the cops," said the woman, then snapped, "The real ones!"

22

"What were you doing with those jerrycans?"

Vesta gave her interrogator the stink eye, which admittedly was a little hard since he was her grandson-in-law and she'd just seen him get married to her beloved granddaughter. Still she thought she did a pretty good job under the circumstances. "I don't know what you're talking about," she said. "What jerrycans?"

Chase's eyes narrowed. He was in full-on interrogation mode, Vesta saw, and she pitied the crooks who had to sit here and submit to this kind of treatment. She was pretty sure they'd all crack under the strain. She wouldn't, of course, since she was a lot tougher than most crooks.

"You were seen inserting four empty yellow jerrycans into a tool shed located on the private property of Mr. and Mrs. Bart and Vanda Dibble. There are three witnesses who saw you: Mr. Bart Dibble, Mrs. Vanda Dibble, and Odelia Poole."

"Frankly there were two more," she said. "Max and Dooley were also there, but I guess they don't count, do they?"

The cop stared at her for a moment. "No," he said finally. "They don't count. So let me ask you again. What were you doing with those four jerrycans? Where did you get them and why were you trying to hide them in the tool shed belonging to the Dibbles?"

In turn, she narrowed her eyes, too. "I plead the fifth."

"This is not a courtroom, Vesta. This is a police interrogation. All I want from you is an answer to a simple question: where the hell did those jerrycans come from?"

She was pretty sure Odelia had already told her husband all about those jerrycans, which made this interview pretty much a waste of time in her view. Still, she wasn't going to incriminate herself. No sirree. So she leaned forward and placed her elbows on the table. "I don't know what the hell you're talking about, Chase."

"We'll see about that," he growled, then abruptly got up and left the room.

"Those intimidation techniques won't work on me, buddy boy!" she shouted. "I know my rights!"

Well, actually she didn't, but at least she knew from watching a ton of Perry Mason shows that it's always better not to talk to the cops.

§

One room over, in interview room number two, Alec Lip was interviewing Scarlett Canyon. Scarlett wasn't entirely at ease. Not that she hadn't been arrested before, because she had, but it still wasn't exactly the kind of thing she enjoyed as a pastime.

"For the last time, Scarlett," said Alec, tapping the table with impatient fingers. "What were you doing with those jerrycans? And is it true you found them at Joshua Curtis's place?"

"Who told you that!" she snapped, then realized she probably shouldn't have said that. In her defense, though, she wasn't exactly a pro at this kind of stuff.

"Look, we've got my mother in the next room, and right now she's probably singing like a canary."

"That's impossible."

"Why? She knows what's good for her."

"No, I mean, Vesta can't sing. So I know you're lying to me right now, Alec Lip," she added, wiggling a reproachful finger in the man's face.

Alec had the decency to wince a little. He probably didn't enjoy raking his mom's best friend over the coals any more than she enjoyed the process of being raked.

Just then, the door opened and Chase stuck his head in. He bent over Alec, and the two men engaged in a whispered conversation that lasted a couple of minutes. Then Alec nodded, and Chase departed.

"Just as I thought," he said. "Vesta is laying it all out for us. Telling the whole story A to Z. Which makes things really difficult for you, Scarlett, I can promise you that."

"What do you mean?"

"She just told my deputy that you're the one who found those jerrycans in Joshua Curtis's garage and that you suggested planting them in that tool shed."

"That's a lie!" Scarlett cried.

"Well, that's what she says. We explained to her exactly what I just explained to you: that only one of you is going to be offered this deal of immunity in exchange for a full confession. Looks like Vesta beat you to it."

She chewed her bottom lip. "Can I think about it?"

Alec slammed his fist on the table. "Thinking time is over, Scarlett! It's now or never! Think on your feet!"

"You're making me very nervous, Alec!" she cried. "And I don't like it when people make me nervous. I get very upset when that happens, and when I get upset I start screaming!"

Alec's face sagged. "Not the screaming," he said. "Please not the screaming."

"I can feel it coming up!" Scarlett warned.

"Please, have mercy," said Alec.

❦

*C*hase had left the room and now returned. Trickery, Vesta understood. Mind games these cops liked to play. But she wasn't going to be fooled by this nonsense. "I want a cup of coffee," she said the moment the burly cop rejoined the interview.

"You can't have one," Chase grunted as he took a seat again.

"I know my rights! I want a cup of coffee!"

"You can have your coffee, but you gotta give me something in return."

"I'm going to file charges against you, Chase Kingsley!"

"Who with?"

"Your wife!"

Chase blanched a little, but held his own. "I have to say, Vesta. I thought you were smarter."

"Oh, yeah?"

"Yeah. Alec told me you're the smartest of the two of you, but so far it looks like it's Scarlett who's winning the race."

"What are you talking about? What race?"

"I told you at the start of this interview how only one of you will be offered a deal. Talk in exchange for immunity. Looks like Scarlett is about to win the big prize. She's singing like a canary in there," he added, jerking his thumb in the direction of the wall, behind which presumably Scarlett was holed up, also being interviewed.

"Ha ha ha," said Vesta.

"What's so funny?"

"You! Everybody knows Scarlett can't sing."

"Well, she's singing right now, spilling the beans. She claims that you stole those jerrycans from Joshua Curtis's garage, after you broke into the guy's house. She also claims that it was your idea to plant those jerrycans in that tool shed, trying to put the blame for those killings on the Dibbles. What do you have to say to that?"

Suddenly a loud scream came from the next room, and Vesta cried, "Is that what you call singing like a canary? You're torturing her, you brute! This is an outrage!"

Chase swallowed away a lump, and just then a knock sounded at the door and Alec strode in. He bent over Chase and started whispering something into his ear.

"What are you two whispering about?" Vesta demanded, but received no response. "Hey, I asked you a question, Alec. You can't do this to me, you know. You can't do this to your little old mother. There are laws against this kind of thing." She suddenly grabbed for her heart. "Owowow," she said. "I just felt a stinging pain in my chest. Ouchie-ouch. Yeah, I think it's my heart. You better call a doctor. And you better start recording my last words, for this is it. When they find my body, you'll be the ones being hauled in front of a jury, who'll wanna know who would treat their feeble old mother like this."

Unfortunately for her the two men blithely ignored her long lament, and then Alec left and Chase stared at her like a cat who's about to eat a canary—the one that had just started singing, presumably.

"What?" said Vesta. "Why are you looking at me like that?"

"You've done it now, Vesta."

"What have I done now?"

"The Chief just told me it's in the bag."

"What's in the bag?"

"The deal! Scarlett just signed a document granting her full immunity in exchange for her confession, and she's put all the blame squarely on you." And to emphasize his words, he poked a finger in Vesta's direction.

"She did what?!"

"She talked! Said this was all your idea!"

"No, she didn't!"

"Oh, yes, she did."

"Look, it may have been my idea," she said, "but Scarlett was in on it from the start. She was there when we broke into the Curtis place, and she searched the upstairs while I searched the downstairs. In fact it was her that found that nude painting of the Melanie Myers woman. Okay, so I found the jerrycans, and so it was my idea to get rid of them, making sure a silly little piece of evidence like that didn't land Odelia's client in the soup. And sure, it was also my idea to plant them at the Dibbles, but Scarlett was with me every step of the way, so she can't go crying wolf now. If she didn't agree, she should have said so!"

"Why did you plant those jerrycans at the Dibbles?"

"Cause they're guilty, Chase! Isn't it obvious? They'd been complaining about that crack house for months, and finally they decided enough was enough. If the cops weren't going to do anything about it, they would take matters into their own hands, and so they torched the place. So what if a couple of drug dealers ended up dead? Good riddance!"

"When we process those jerrycans, are we going to find your fingerprints? Or Scarlett's?"

"What do you think I am? A rookie? I wore gloves the entire time, dumbo."

He ignored this slur as he jotted down a note. "Did you take anything else from the Curtis place apart from those jerrycans?"

"No, nothing. I wanted to take that painting, but it didn't seem like a good idea."

"And why is that?"

"Too heavy! Do you think I want a hernia? Those jerrycans were easy. They were empty."

"Empty, huh?" said Chase as he jotted down another note.

"Sure. Which is why I figured you guys would probably use them as some kind of evidence against Odelia's client."

"You keep referring to Joshua Curtis as Odelia's client. But he isn't her client, is he? Just a guy who asked her to do him a favor."

"If you're gonna get all nitpicky about it, sure," she allowed. Then she smiled. "So now do I get the deal or what?"

Chase got up and said, stony-faced, "What deal?"

"Hey, you said there was a deal on the table!" she cried as he left the room. "I want my deal!"

It took her another couple of minutes of sitting in silence to realize that A) there was no deal. B) there never was a deal. And C) she'd just been played!

e were sitting in Odelia's car, on what is commonly termed a stakeout, watching the house that belongs to Joshua Curtis. There was a lot of police activity going on: cops were walking in and out of the house, carrying boxes and crates and all kinds of stuff.

"What is going on?" Odelia said.

Our human was a little frustrated, I could tell. She'd walked up to the cops and asked them what was happening, and what they were dragging out of the house, but they were all under strict instructions from her uncle not to divulge anything about the case to her.

"Maybe you guys can go in there and take a look?" she finally suggested.

It had been an eventful evening already, what with Gran and Scarlett being arrested in flagrante delicto, for trying to plant stolen evidence in the Dibbles' tool shed, and probably for trespassing, as I don't think they'd asked permission before they snuck in.

"Let's go, Dooley," I said as Odelia opened the door.

So we tripped across the street to find out what was

going on. Already we knew that four jerrycans had been found in Joshua's garage, but now it looked like more stuff was going to be used to tie Odelia's client to this triple homicide.

Dooley, who'd been glancing upwards, now asked, "Do you think storks work at night, Max? Or do you think they sleep?"

"I thought you'd finally dropped the whole stork thing?"

"Well, I know that Odelia says she wants to wait to have babies, but it's not up to her, is it? When that stork decides to drop a baby in her lap, he's going to drop that baby in her lap, whether she likes it or not."

"It doesn't work like that, Dooley."

"No, but it does, Max! It happens all the time on General Hospital. Even to people who aren't even married. One of the doctors had an affair with a nurse and one morning she came into his office and announced that she was pregnant. And he was married to another person! So either that stork made a big mistake, or storks simply don't care whether a person is ready or not. They just deliver those babies anyway."

"Sure, Dooley," I said as we watched the cops work like beavers—or glorified movers. When all this was over, and Joshua was let out of jail again, he'd have a hard time recognizing his place, with all the stuff that had been removed from it.

"I have a theory," said Dooley now, visibly pleased with himself.

"What is your theory?" I asked, curious in spite of myself.

"Well, I think that the International Association of Storks is tasked with the important task that there should always be a certain number of babies in the world, so they simply go around distributing them. Now if a person is ready to have a baby, so much the better. But even if they're not, those babies have to be placed somewhere, right? So they are going to be placed, whether the people getting them are ready or not."

"Right," I said dubiously as I watched Sarah Flunk, one of Odelia's uncle's officers, carry a very large portrait out of the house, along with another cop. The portrait portrayed Melanie Myers in the nude, and was a vivid depiction of her likeness.

"Hey, that's that painting of Melanie Myers without any clothes on," said Dooley, momentarily distracted from his stork theory. "You still haven't explained to me why she's not wearing any clothes, Max."

"She probably forgot to get dressed," I said. "It happens. Let's go inside and have a closer look."

"But who's going to watch for the stork?"

"Storks don't work at night, Dooley," I said. "They're like most people: they work nine to five and then they take a load off. Let's go."

Much relieved, Dooley traipsed after me as we entered the house.

We quickly made our way upstairs, where all the activity seemed to be focused, and found ourselves in a small room adjacent to Joshua's bedroom.

"Oh, my God," said Dooley. "Will you look at that."

I was looking at that, and it became clear to me that Joshua Curtis had some serious issues: everywhere we looked the smiling face of Melanie Myers greeted us. From pictures hanging on the walls, to painted portraits, to sculpted busts and even a life-sized statue literally placed on a pedestal, LED lights illuminating it from below. There was even one of those small bubbling water features, with Melanie clearly recognizable in the cherub pouring water from her pitcher and looking entirely too happy as she did.

"I think Joshua really likes Melanie," Dooley said. "Like, really really likes her."

"Yeah, a little too much, I would say."

Just then, Chase came walking in, followed by Uncle Alec. They looked around and shook their collective heads, then Chase said, "This is just evidence overload, Chief."

"Talk about an open-and-shut case," his superior officer agreed. "Holy hell, what are those two doing here?"

Since he was staring straight at us, I immediately assumed he was referring to Dooley and myself, so I gave him my best smile and said, "Top of the morning to you, Chief."

But of course he couldn't understand a word I said. Also, it was mid-afternoon at that point, so my greeting was probably out of place. At any rate, he was glowering at us now, clearly not all that happy with our presence at the scene.

"I can't go anywhere without these two spying on me!" he cried, shaking an irate fist. "Pretty soon they'll be in my bedroom, watching me sleep! I'll wake up in the middle of the night and there will be two pairs of cats eyes looking at me from the foot of the bed!"

"We would never do that," I assured the big guy.

"No, we like to sleep at the foot of our own human's bed," Dooley added.

"And watch her sleep."

"It's too much!" Uncle Alec cried.

"They're just cats, Chief," Chase said.

"I know they're just cats, but they're freaking me out."

"They're just doing what Odelia told them to," Chase added as he gestured to the door with a slight shake of the head.

I got his drift immediately, and both Dooley and myself sidled away to the door, keeping our eyes peeled just in case Uncle Alec went full-berserk and launched himself at us. He had that look, you know. That look people get who are about to go cuckoo.

"Look, they're going already," said Chase.

"Probably to go and tell Odelia all about what we discovered here."

"Oh, I'm sure she knows all about it from Vesta and Scarlett."

"More spies! I'm surrounded by spies!" Uncle Alec screamed, sounding like a Roman emperor now, surrounded by wannabe Senate assassins.

"You shouldn't see them as spies so much as helpful contributors," Chase tried. "We all want the same thing, Chief."

"And what's that? To drive me nuts?"

"To solve this case."

"Well, your wife sure has a strange way to go about it, and so does my mom and her friend." He dragged a hand through his modest mane. "I swear to God, Chase, if this keeps up I'm going to slam an injunction on them."

"On who?"

"All of them! My mom, Scarlett, Odelia, and especially those darn cats!"

When we arrived back at the car, to report back to Odelia, we didn't come bearing gifts, but more like stink bombs.

"Looks like Joshua is guilty after all, huh?" she said finally, when we'd painted a colorful word picture of Joshua Curtis's inner sanctum—his shrine to Melanie Myers.

"Yeah, looks like," I agreed.

"Have you seen the stork?" asked Dooley, glancing up nervously.

"I told you already, Dooley," I said. "Storks don't work at night. They sleep."

"Oh, right," said Dooley, relaxing.

"Well, I guess that does it," said Odelia. "Game over. Joshua Curtis was in love with Melanie to such an extent that he decided to kill the man she was having an affair with. Though I still don't get why he hired me."

"So he could stay out of the picture?" I suggested. "He wanted you to snap a couple of pictures of the man she was seeing, and ask you to go and talk to Melanie. That way Melanie would break off the affair, and Joshua wouldn't have to get involved."

"But then why did he decide to kill the guy? And just after I told him the affair was over. That Franklin had ended things." She shook her head. "It just doesn't make sense."

24

*A*fter the long day we'd had, filled with emotion and not a small degree of strife, I was glad that it was time for cat choir again, my favorite entertainment of an evening.

Odelia had dropped us off near the park, and when we arrived at the playground that serves as the backdrop for our nightly rehearsal sessions with the other cats of Hampton Cove, we saw that the showdown had already begun: Shanille was positioned on one side of the playground, near the jungle gym, where a handful of cats were listening to her speech about the importance of respect for one's elders, while Harriet was located on top of the slide, a bunch of cats listening to her speech about the importance of respecting one's peers, especially when they are right and you are wrong.

"They're not going to fight again, are they?" asked Dooley, as we took position somewhere in the middle between the two separate camps.

"I think they might just fight with words today?" I said, though I wasn't entirely sanguine, I must admit. Harriet and

Shanille both have a volatile streak, and just might go paw to paw again. Which would turn cat choir into fight club, which wasn't the idea.

Brutus came over to talk to us, and I could see from his puckered brow and the worried expression on his face that he wasn't liking this any more than we did.

"I tried to stop her," he announced sullenly, "but she wouldn't hear of it. I told her, okay, so maybe Shanille was out of line, but then you should try to be the grownup here. After all, there's nothing to gain by pushing this thing."

"Unfortunately Harriet is not the kind of cat who will back down," I said. "And neither is Shanille."

"Is she going to put it to a vote?" asked Dooley, turning his head like a spectator at a tennis match, looking from Harriet to Shanille as they both seemed to go from strength to strength—oratorically speaking.

"Yeah, she wants to settle this thing once and for all," Brutus confirmed.

"So... what are we supposed to vote about?" I asked.

"She's going to try to push Shanille out of cat choir," said Brutus in a grave tone.

"No way!"

"Yes, way. She wants to take control, so that something like this will never happen again."

"Oh, dear."

"But I don't want to vote for one or the other, Max," said Dooley. "I like Harriet, but I like Shanille, too."

"Plus, I don't think Harriet would make a good choir director," I surmised. "Frankly I think if she goes through with this, cat choir just might split in two: Shanille will take her followers to a different part of the park, and then there will be two cat choirs."

"I'm afraid that just might be the case," said Brutus somberly.

"But I don't want two cat choirs," said Dooley. "I like the fact that we all come together here night after night, and that we all get along!"

"Yeah, well, tell that to Shanille and Harriet," said Brutus. "Clearly they don't get along."

"But…"

Just then, Harriet raised her voice. "Cats of cat choir, the time has come to take a stand: do you really want to keep on living under the dictatorship of Shanille? Or do you want your freedom, under my leadership? It's your choice, and so choose wisely!"

"Dear friends!" Shanille yelled, summoning for silence, "don't listen to my opponent. She doesn't know what she's talking about. She's disrespectful, she's mean, and she's a bully. And I for one feel that we should say no to bullies and therefore start a procedure to expel Harriet from our community once and for all."

"But then who's going to sing the soprano parts?" a voice from the crowd yelled.

"Yeah, I like those sopranos!" another insisted.

"Thank you so, so much," Harriet said, simpering a little. "Look, if you want to hear my sopranos you can hear them every night from now on, and not just when Shanille allows them. In fact you can listen to my sweet voice all the time, if you vote for me."

"If you want tyranny to get a kick in the teeth, you'll vote for me," Shanille snapped.

"Free Cat Snax for all!" Harriet countered.

"Don't listen to her!" said Shanille. "She'll promise you Cat Snax today and eat them all herself tomorrow. Because that's the kind of cat Harriet is: selfish!"

"Oh, shut up, Shanille."

"No, you shut up!"

"Oh, dear," I murmured.

"If this keeps up," said Dooley, "the stork will be scared off by all the yelling."

Soon it was time to vote, and oddly enough the electorate was split right down the middle: Harriet got half of the vote, and so did Shanille.

"I demand a recount!" Harriet cried. "This can't be right!"

"Yeah, let's have a recount!" Shanille agreed. "This can't possibly be right!"

After a few tense moments, it turned out that the vote was exactly the same as the first time, so it was finally decided that a committee would be created that would try and figure a way out of this stalemate. So more voting took place, and suddenly I found myself the leader of this commission.

Yikes!

My fellow committee members were Dooley, Brutus, Kingman and Buster, and before long we were engaged in a tense meeting trying to resolve this remarkable situation.

"I think we should probably have a dual leadership of cat choir from now on," Kingman suggested.

"You mean put both Harriet and Shanille in charge?" I asked.

"Exactly! It would solve all of our problems. They could be co-directors. Everybody happy!"

"I don't think so," said Brutus, once more providing the gloomy note. "Harriet is not the kind of cat who's great at cooperation. Put her and Shanille in charge and they'll end up fighting tooth and claw."

"I think he's right," said Buster. "They simply are incapable of sharing the power."

"So what do we do then?" asked Kingman. "Any other suggestions?"

"We could alternate," said Brutus. "One night will be

Shanille night, and the next will be Harriet's turn. That way they both get what they want."

"Not entirely," I said. "On the nights Harriet is in charge Shanille will do everything in her power to sabotage the rehearsals, and vice versa. We'll end up with a protracted war."

"So then what?"

Frankly we were all stumped and out of ideas. So we decided to sleep on it and reconvene the next day. It sure was a tough proposition.

And as we walked home that night, Dooley said, "I'm worried, Max."

"Me, too," I admitted.

"I mean, what will the stork think? He's probably going to be scared off by all the bickering and fighting. And then what?"

I decided to settle this thing once and for all. "Look, Dooley, Odelia has clearly said that she and Chase don't want to start a family right now. They have plenty of time and so let's give them that time, all right? The stork will just have to wait," I added, anticipating his next remark.

He thought about this for a moment, then finally nodded. "All right, Max. We have to respect Odelia's wishes. The stork will just have to wait."

"Exactly."

"I mean, after all it's up to Odelia and Chase. They're the ones who get to decide."

"Absolutely!" I said, much relieved he was taking this stance.

"On the other hand," he said, "we have to think of that poor stork, too."

"What?"

"Well, we do. Storks are hard-working birds. They have to fly around carrying babies all the time. And you know babies are heavy, Max. They come in at seven or eight pounds. Can you imagine that poor stork, flying all the way out here, carrying a seven-pound baby in its beak, having to turn back? I don't think we can do that to the poor bird."

"But..."

"No, I think Odelia will just have to change her mind, and I'm going to have a long talk with her the first chance I get."

"But, Dooley!"

"Storks have rights, too, Max!"

Oh, dear, oh, dear, oh, dear.

25

Odelia was having breakfast when her mom and dad suddenly stormed into the house, looking perturbed. Marge, who was Odelia's lookalike, only twenty years her senior, and Tex, her white-haired amiable doctor husband, immediately got down to brass tacks.

"Is it true that your grandmother was arrested last night?" asked Mom.

"Um, yeah, I guess she was," said Odelia, who'd been enjoying a cup of strong black coffee and a Nutella sandwich. "But they let her walk as soon as she confessed."

"Confessed!" Mom cried, raising her eyes heavenward and placing a hand to her chest in a gesture of extreme agitation.

"But what was she arrested for in the first place is what I'd like to know," said Odelia's dad as he took the Nutella pot, a spoon, and dipped it into the pot with the air of a man digging for treasure.

"It's a long story," said Odelia. "Do you really want to know?"

"Yes! Of course we want to know why a woman who's

living under our roof got arrested!" said Mom.

"Well…"

"Howdy folks," said Chase, as he came ambling down the stairs, looking chipper and bright.

"Is it true that you arrested my mother last night?" Mom demanded, not looking exactly like a loving mother-in-law should regard her newly acquired son-in-law.

"Why, yeah, I guess I did," said Chase a little sheepishly.

"And did you grill her hard?" asked Dad with some relish.

"Tex!" Mom cried.

"I'm sorry. I meant: did she confess to whatever it was she was up to?"

"Oh, yeah, she confessed all right," said Chase with a slight grin as he, in turn, filled a cup with delicious black brew and took a seat at the kitchen counter.

"What did she do?!" Mom practically yelled.

"Well, she was caught trying to plant four stolen jerrycans in the tool shed belonging to an old couple," Chase explained.

"She did what?! Oh, my God!" Again the eyes went heavenward and the hand desperately clutched at the chest, as if trying to draw comfort from the gesture.

"It's fine, Mom," said Odelia. "The Dibbles aren't pressing charges, are they, Chase?"

"No, I don't think they will. The Chief managed to talk them out of it. They were pretty eager to, though. Apparently people aren't happy when two burglars sneak into their backyard at night and try to plant stolen evidence in a murder case. Go figure."

"This evidence was stolen?" asked Dad, delightedly licking from his spoon and helping himself to a cup of coffee. He seemed to enjoy the episode tremendously.

"Yeah, they stole the jerrycans from the house of Joshua Curtis, suspect in a murder case. They figured they were doing Odelia a favor, while in fact they weren't doing anyone any favors at all, least of all themselves. But we got it all squared away and the evidence is safely secured, and will be processed for fingerprints and the like."

"But why? Why is she doing this?!" Mom cried.

"Because I wanted to save Odelia's client, of course," a voice spoke from the sliding glass door, which had opened and closed to allow the final member of the Poole family to join this impromptu breakfast meeting.

"Thanks for nothing by the way, Gran," said Odelia. "I never asked you to steal evidence for me. And now Uncle Alec thinks I'm trying to sabotage his investigation and won't let me come anywhere near the case."

"Look, I'm sure Joshua Curtis will have a perfectly good explanation for why those empty jerrycans were in his garage."

"Actually he doesn't," said Chase. "I interviewed him again last night, and he claims he's never seen those jerrycans before, nor did he put them in his garage. He claims someone must have planted them."

"And did they?" asked Odelia, interested in anything Joshua had to say.

"Of course not. He's just trying to wriggle himself out of this thing."

"That does seem rather like a silly thing to do though, don't you think?" said Dad.

"What does, Dad?" asked Chase as he took a seat next to his father-in-law.

"Well, if this Joshua Curtis really did torch the place, and killed those people, wouldn't he have made sure not to leave the jerrycans lying around his garage? Murderers usually try to conceal the evidence of their crimes, don't they? I mean, I'm not a murderer myself, so I can't speak from experience, but that seems to be one of the first rules of murder: get rid of the evidence."

"See?" said Gran. "I knew he didn't do it!"

"He did do it," said Chase. "No question about his guilt at this point. As to why he didn't get rid of the evidence." He shrugged. "When you've been a cop for as long as I have, Dad, you understand that there are clever criminals, and not-so-clever ones. And clearly Joshua belongs in the last category."

"He gave me the impression of being very clever," Odelia countered.

"Yeah, well, as I see it the man let his emotions get the better of him. He was so in love with Melanie Myers that the idea that another man was putting his hands on her made him so angry he just had to kill him. And so he didn't think things through."

"I think you're wrong, Chase," said Gran. "I think you and Alec got this whole thing backward, and because you're so focused on Joshua, you're letting the real killer walk."

"Ma, please promise me never to get arrested again," said Odelia's mom. "It's not a good look. We all have to live in this town, and you know how people like to talk."

"Oh, let them talk. I know I was doing the right thing."

"You were caught stealing!"

"Caught planting stolen evidence," Chase quietly corrected her.

"I was trying to help your daughter!"

"Please don't help me anymore, Gran," Odelia pleaded. "Your help is not helping me."

"So this is the kind of thanks I get! After all that I've done for you?! Anyway, I can't stand around here arguing. I've got things to do and people to see. So I wish you all a good day, and don't call me—I'll call you." And with these words, she was off, leaving a lot of bemused glances to rake her retreating back.

"ax?"

"Mh."

"Max!"

I opened one eye and saw that Harriet desired speech with me.

"Yes?" I said, and yawned prodigiously, stretching myself in the process. I'd been quietly dozing in a corner of Odelia's office, while my human worked away at a couple of articles: one about two elderly ladies being arrested for trespassing—no mention was made of the jerrycans, at the request of the police department—and one about the arrest of a suspect in the case of arson that had claimed the lives of three tragic victims. Suffice it to say she had her work cut out for her.

"You have to do something!" Harriet said.

"What," I said, "do I have to do?"

"You have to convince the other members of the commission to let that vote swing my way!"

"What vote?" And then I remembered. "Oh, that vote. Look, Harriet, I can't let the vote swing your way. We're a neutral commission and we're going to find a solution that is beneficial to everyone."

"But Max—you're my friend! My best friend!"

"I know I'm your friend, Harriet, but Shanille is also my friend, and I'm going to be fair and square about this thing."

"Look, if you do me this one little favor I'm going to make it worth your while."

"How are you going to make it worth my while?" I said, wondering what she'd come up with.

"Well, I'll..." She paused, thinking hard. "I'll, um..."

"Yes?"

"I could give you some of my food," she suggested. "Some of my Cat Snax. In fact why don't I give you all of my Cat Snax for the next three months—six months," she quickly interposed when she saw the dubious expression on my face. "A year!"

"Look, I don't need your Cat Snax, Harriet. I have plenty of Cat Snax of my own. And what's more, I still have to live in this town, and if I'm going to be corrupted by your offer I won't be able to show my face around here again. And neither, I have to warn you, will you."

"But I have to win this thing! I threw down the gauntlet and if I don't win now cats will laugh at me—I'll be the laughingstock of the whole town!"

"You probably should have thought of that before you started quarreling."

"Oh, Max, you have to help me. You simply have to make the vote swing my way. I need to get rid of Shanille."

"I'm sorry, Harriet."

Her expression turned hostile. "And here I thought you were my friend!"

"I am your friend. And I'm trying to do the right thing. And you know what would help a lot? If you'd go up to Shanille and apologized."

"What?! Me apologize to that harridan! Never!"

I watched her stalk off and wondered, frankly, how we were ever going to get out of this mess, when suddenly the door swung open and a woman entered. I didn't recognize her, which is saying something, as I know a lot of people in this town.

"Miss Poole?" the woman said. "Miss Odelia Poole?"

Odelia looked up from her laptop. "Yes?"

"My name is Francine Ritter. I used to be married to Franklin Harrison—the man who was killed the other night in a fire?"

"Oh, of course. Please take a seat, Mrs. Ritter," said Odelia. "What can I do for you?"

Mrs. Ritter was a fair-haired woman in her late thirties, dressed in a purple tunic and black leggings. Her hair was frizzy and she looked a little unkempt.

"The thing is, my ex-husband hadn't paid child support in months, and I'd been hounding him to come through."

"You and Franklin had kids?"

"Yeah, two little girls. And ever since we got divorced it's been really tough, and Franklin didn't make it any easier, with his refusal to pay for the girls."

"Any reason he refused to pay?"

"Plain meanness, I guess," said the woman with an embarrassed smile. "Frankly I didn't know what kind of man I married until a couple of months into the marriage. When we were dating he was the sweetest guy on the planet, always buying me gifts and showering me with affection. But after the girls were born, he seemed to lose interest in the life of a married man and father. He started going out more and staying away longer, and didn't take up his share of the work in raising the girls. And when I discovered he was having affairs with other women, I finally decided that enough was enough."

"As I understand it Franklin died destitute," said Odelia. "His dad cut him off, and he was living in a squat house after he was evicted from his apartment for not making rent."

"I know. I heard about that. But he was still the father of my girls, and he didn't keep his end of the bargain, so now I'm trying to talk to his brother. Set up a meeting. They need to take their responsibility and step up. But so far they've been ignoring me. They won't take my calls, they won't answer my letters."

"Can't you hire an attorney? Go to court?"

Mrs. Ritter blushed. "I'm afraid I don't have the money, Miss Poole. The Harrisons are very wealthy people, and I feel —I feel I don't stand much of a chance. The arrangement was between Franklin and myself. They'll simply argue they have no obligations to me."

"I understand," said Odelia. "So what do you suggest?"

"Couldn't you perhaps talk to them? Maybe they'll listen to you. Or you could threaten to write an article."

Odelia nodded thoughtfully.

"You could write how one of the richest families in town refuses to take care of their own. I may be divorced, but my girls are still Herbert and Ruth's granddaughters. It's disgraceful the way they simply cut them out of their lives like that."

"Your girls haven't seen their grandparents?"

"Not since the divorce."

"That's pretty harsh," said Odelia.

"Just call it what it is: cruel."

"I'll see what I can do," said Odelia. "But I can't promise you anything."

"If you could just talk to them. I know they'll listen to you. They have a business to run. They may be heartless and cruel, but they are also afraid of negative publicity, so…"

When the woman left the office, I decided to follow her

out. I hadn't seen Dooley in a while, and I had the feeling he might be outside, keeping an eye out for that elusive and hard-working stork who'd been lugging Odelia's babies around ever since she got married.

Dooley was indeed sitting outside on the sidewalk, his eyes peeled as he kept a close watch on the skies above Hampton Cove.

"Any sign of the stork?" I asked him.

"He isn't showing his face," he lamented. "Do you think something scared him off?"

"Yeah, that must be it," I said as I took a seat next to my friend.

Francine Ritter had crossed the street, and was walking along the sidewalk when suddenly she halted in her tracks, and seemed to stiffen.

A man came from the other direction, and he, too, halted, then quickly made an about-face and started walking back the way he'd come.

"Marvin!" she yelled. "Marvin, wait!"

The man stopped and turned, and for a moment they engaged in tense conversation. I couldn't hear what they were saying, but from their body language it was obvious these people weren't friends. There was a lot of angry yelling from Mrs. Ritter's side, and stony-faced looks from this Marvin person's side. And as I watched, suddenly I recognized the man as Marvin Harrison, who Mrs. Ritter had been trying to get hold of about that missing child support.

Clearly Marvin wasn't happy to bump into his former sister-in-law, and I didn't think she'd be able to extract a lot of money from him.

The meeting finally came to an abrupt end, and Marvin crossed the street, then came walking in our direction. A nice black Tesla stood parked at the curb, and I had the feeling it could just be Mr. Harrison's ride.

Just as he reached our side of the street, he turned and glanced back in the direction of Mrs. Ritter. And as he watched her stalk off, an angry spring in her step, I thought I saw a distinct look of fear in the man's eye. Clearly he wasn't happy about this surprise meeting. Mrs. Ritter was correct in assuming the Harrisons abhorred negative publicity.

27

"Why is Dooley looking at the sky the whole time, Max?" asked Odelia as she glanced back at her cats through the rearview mirror.

"He's still looking for your stork," Max explained. "He feels that bird has worked so hard, and come so far carrying that baby—"

"Or babies," Dooley corrected him.

"—or babies, that it would be very unkind to send him all the way back to... Where did you say he came from, Dooley?"

"Baby-land, of course. Everybody knows that, Max."

"It's the land where they make the babies," Max said.

"Oh-kay," said Odelia, a smile on her face. Dooley was so sweet. She didn't have the heart to tell him that storks didn't make home deliveries, and that babies didn't come from baby-land.

They were on their way to the vast estate—or at least she assumed it was an estate, and vast—of the Harrison family, to argue the case of Francine Ritter's missing child support checks. It was the least she could do for the poor woman, she thought. And it would give her an opportunity to meet Franklin Harrison's family. She felt a little bad now, for taking on Joshua Curtis's case. Clearly the man was guilty after all, and working to prove his innocence had probably been a misguided effort on her part.

They arrived at the entrance to what indeed was an estate, and she announced her arrival to the intercom located outside the tall gate. The gate swung open, and she directed her aged old car along the drive toward a sizable mansion and parked in the circular drive, her tires crunching the nice yellow gravel that looked like brown sugar.

"You know the drill, you guys," she said as she opened the door. "You snoop around while I talk to the people in charge of this place."

"Will do," said Max, and both cats hopped out, Dooley keeping a close eye on the skies all the while.

The front door opened the moment she set foot on the first step of a granite landing and for a moment she was too startled to proceed: the man who greeted her at the door was... Franklin Harrison. "Hi," said the apparition. "I'm Marvin Harrison. And you are Odelia Poole, of course. I read your articles all the time, Miss Poole. Please come in."

He was a little stiff and serious, and his glasses gave him a bookish look, but otherwise he was the spitting image of his now dearly departed brother.

"You and Franklin were twins?" she couldn't help blurting out.

"Yeah, we were identical twins," Marvin confirmed as he led the way into a sitting room. "Born just two minutes apart, or at least that's what my mother claims. Please take a seat. I'll go and get Mother."

She did as he suggested, but not before walking around the room and taking in the scene: the floor was marble, with a nice thick rug for warmth, and there were white columns supporting a ceiling that was adorned with intricate mold-ings. Paintings of horses decorated the walls, and large picture windows offered a terrific view of spreading greenery surrounding the house. Not a bad place to grow up, she thought. Strange, then, that Marvin's brother had so gone off the rails, and met a terrible death.

She finally took a seat, and moments later Marvin returned with a matronly woman, her hair piled high on her head, dressed in long flowing robes that gave her a slightly oriental look, and wearing a stern look on her broad face. She lowered herself onto an upholstered chair and regarded Odelia like the Queen would regard a royal subject.

Marvin, dressed in a turtleneck and corduroy slacks, remained standing next to his mother's chair. "You wished to talk to me?" said the woman a little haughtily, not exactly overflowing with joy about Odelia's visit.

"Yes, as a matter of fact I did. Francine Ritter came to see me this morning."

Mother and son shared a look of concern.

"Yes?" said Mrs. Harrison a little stiffishly.

"It would appear she hasn't received child support for the last six months, and she asked me to come and have a word with you, and maybe try to find a way to sort things out."

"There's nothing to sort out," Mrs. Harrison snapped. "We don't owe that woman anything."

"But she's the mother of your grandchildren."

"That may be so but she's also the main cause of my son's ruin."

"Mother, maybe we should first listen to what Miss Poole has to say," Marvin suggested. He seemed more forthcoming about his ex-sister-in-law's predicament than his mother.

"I will not," said his mother, "listen to any of this nonsense. I blame that woman for Franklin's death, and so she gets nothing—not a cent!"

"Why do you feel she's responsible for your son's death?" asked Odelia.

"Because ever since he met Francine, Franklin started down the path that led to his ruin." Her face softened as she gazed upon a framed picture of her son. "Franklin was always such a sweet boy. We had high hopes for him, Herbert and I. But after he met Francine he changed. Gone was the fun-loving boy I knew and loved. He started drinking and using illegal substances and God knows what else. I didn't recognize my own son!"

"Mother," said Marvin warningly.

"No, Marvin, someone has to tell that woman what's what, and clearly she's chosen Miss Poole as her emissary." She turned back to Odelia. "Is she taking us to court?"

"I'm not sure," said Odelia. "I think she would prefer to deal with this amicably."

"Amicably! There can be no amicability between us and Francine, Miss Poole."

"But what about your granddaughters?" said Odelia, taking out her phone. She held it out, showing a picture of the two girls. They looked like two blond-haired little angels.

Mrs. Harrison momentarily seemed to relent, but then her expression hardened and she said, emphatically, "Those girls are not my blood." And with these words, she majestically rose, and walked out.

Marvin took the seat his mother had vacated and gave Odelia an apologetic look. "I'm sorry," he said, "but Mother feels very strongly about this. I talked to her before, and she feels that when Francine left Franklin she also forfeited any right she might have had to his money—our money. And now that he's dead, well..."

"But surely she is entitled to the child support your brother owed her?"

"Franklin didn't pay because Franklin couldn't pay," said

Marvin quietly. "My brother had gone down a very dark path, Miss Poole, but I'm sure you're aware of that. He lost his standing in the community and his position as part of this family. My father...." He glanced up at the ceiling, then continued, "My father decided to cut him off six months ago, because he felt that Franklin had become an embarrassment, and didn't want anything more to do with him."

"How is your father?" she asked solicitously. "Even though he was unhappy with your brother he still must have been devastated when he heard about what happened."

"We haven't told him. We're afraid that if he finds out it will kill him." He took a deep breath, and stared out the window. Odelia could see that the death of his brother had affected him powerfully. To lose a sibling is an awful thing, but to lose a twin, she knew, was like losing part of oneself. "Father isn't well, you see. In fact he's pretty much at death's door. He's a good deal older than Mother. Mother is sixty-six, but Father is eighty-seven, and he's been ill for quite some time. He's strong, and he's holding on for as long as he can, but we're afraid that a shock like that would be the end. So we prefer to keep him in the dark. Let him think Franklin is still out there, up to his usual mischief."

"Was he always like that, your brother?"

A smile lit up the man's face. "Oh, yes. Franklin and I may be twins, but we couldn't be more different. He's always been a troublemaker. Even as a young boy he used to run around setting off firecrackers in the kitchen or shooting at windows with a BB gun. He'd drive our parents crazy. I was always the bookish kid, never happier than with my nose stuck in a book in some corner of this big rambling place we are lucky enough to call home." He turned back to Odelia. "Don't get me wrong, Miss Poole. I loved my brother. I absolutely did. But he was a handful, and maybe he's better off now, wherever he is. He was definitely a tortured soul, and the last couple of years even more so than before."

"Do you agree with your mother that Francine is to blame for his behavior?"

"No, absolutely not," he said emphatically. "In fact I think Francine had a positive influence on him. While they were together he was doing much better. Unfortunately he couldn't accept the responsibility of fatherhood, and of raising a family, and so he escaped, and soon was up to his old tricks again. Sleeping around, doing drugs…"

"Did you know he was living in a squat house?"

"No, I didn't know that," said Marvin softly. "He'd clearly gone downhill since the last time I saw him. Even though Father had cut him off, we still met up from time to time, and so did mother—behind Father's back, of course." He smiled a small smile and picked up the portrait of his brother. "All I can think is that he's in a better place now."

*A*fter we got out of the car we looked around for any pets we could talk to. Odelia likes to get the inside track of any place she visits, and the best way to accomplish that is through us. People might keep a lot of secrets from other people, but they can't keep secrets from their pets, and since those pets usually like to gab as much as humans do, we usually get an earful.

"Is that a horse, Max?" asked Dooley suddenly, indicating a small pen where a pony stood grazing languidly.

"I think that's a pony," I said.

We walked over to the pony, and it looked up from its perusal of its supply of grass. "Hey, there," it said as soon as we hove into view. "Are you guys the new pets? I don't think I've ever seen you before. Are you Marvin's? Or his mom's? Gee, I just wish they'd get another pony. It's not much fun being all by my lonesome out here, you know. I could really use a friend to talk to. Shoot the shit. Chew the cud. Though personally I don't chew cud—I'm not a cow, you see. I'm a pony, if you hadn't noticed. So who are you guys?"

"He's a big talker, Max," Dooley whispered.

"Yeah, he is," I whispered back. Which is a good thing, of course. Nothing worse than a pet who won't talk to us.

"We're not the new pets," I said, "either of Marvin or his mother."

"We're Odelia Poole's cats," said Dooley. "And she's just visiting your humans—those are your humans in there, I suppose?"

"Yeah, they got me for Franklin's kids, but then Franklin got divorced and the girls haven't been here since. Ruth doesn't like the girls' mother, see. She thinks she did something to make Franklin leave her, and go down a path of self-destruction, and so she refuses to talk to her anymore, or the girls. Which is a pity, as I don't have anyone to play with now. The girls were fun. Jaime and Marje. They're twins, just like Franklin and Marvin. Maybe the twin gene runs in the family? I don't know. You tell me."

Unfortunately I had no expert opinion on the twin gene topic, so I decided to skip this one. Instead I explained, "Odelia is here to plead Francine's case. She wants to make sure the girls are taken care of, since Franklin wasn't the best at that kind of thing."

"He refused to pay child support," Dooley clarified.

"Yeah, Franklin was what you might call an irresponsible father," the pony agreed. "In fact I don't think he even liked to be a dad. Which is weird, cause these girls are really nice, and how can anyone not like them, you know? But hey, I guess that's just the way it goes, you know. My name is Jane, by the way—what's yours?"

"I'm Max," I said, "and this is my friend Dooley."

"Nice to meet you, Max and Dooley. So did you know Franklin?"

"No, we didn't," I admitted.

"He was a little weird. Selfish. Wasn't interested in anyone but himself. And that included me! He didn't like ponies. Had no use for them, he once told me." Jane shook her head. "So not a nice person." She then ripped off a big chunk of grass with her tongue and started chewing. "Too bad he died, though. He wasn't nice, but that doesn't mean he had to die."

"How do you know he died?"

"Duh. I may be the only pony here, but that doesn't mean I don't have friends, you guys." Just then, a bird landed on her back and started twittering like crazy. "This is Jake," said the pony affectionately. "He brings me all the latest news from town."

The bird took off again, and I asked, "So did your friend Jake tell you what happened to Franklin?"

"Yeah, he did. Died in a fire, right? In some crumbling old building? Sad way to go." She shivered. "To die by fire. Terrible business. I hate fires, you know. Always afraid one will start and it will kill me."

"I don't think you've got anything to worry about, Jane," I said.

"That's what you think, Max. There was a fire here a while back. I could see the smoke. I thought that was it. I was going to be for it. But luckily it went out again. Probably Chester burning some old leaves. At least that's what Jake told me later."

"Chester? Who's Chester?" I asked.

"Chester Sosnoski. The gardener. He's great. Keeps the place looking shipshape. He's probably the best gardener for miles around. Or at least that's what Ruth says."

I glanced around, and had to admit that Chester did a great job: the grass was cut to perfection, the flowerbeds were all immaculate, with not a weed in sight, and all in all the gardens looked more like a golf club than our own backyard. Then again, the Harrisons probably had a lot more spending power and could get the best gardener that money can buy. We have to make do with Gran occasionally remembering she's supposed to have a green thumb, and Tex finding the time to mow the lawn.

We said our goodbyes to Jane the talking pony, and decided to go for a little stroll, especially after learning that there were no other pets around, so it was frankly pointless for us to enter the house, since there would be no kibble to be had, unfortunately.

And we'd walked perhaps half a mile or so when we came upon a small structure that at one time had been an animal shed, but that now showed signs of fire damage.

"This might be what Jane said she saw," Dooley intimated.

"Yeah, might be," I said, "though it does look as if this fire happened a long time ago."

"They probably want to tear it down but haven't gotten round to it."

Just then, a man dressed in rubber boots and a green anorak that had seen better days came stomping up, accompanied by a man who was also in rubber boots but otherwise immaculately dressed.

"So this is where they want the pagoda," the man in the anorak said.

"Excellent location, Chester," said the well-dressed man. "I'll get busy on the plans."

"She wants it ready as soon as possible."

"Not a problem. I'll make it a priority."

"I think that man is an architect," I explained to Dooley, "and that man is Chester the gardener."

Looked like I was right: the dilapidated structure had been earmarked for destruction, a nice pagoda about to take its place.

"Let's get back to the house," I suggested. "Odelia will probably be finished by now."

And so we set a course back to the house. Suddenly the man named Chester uttered a loud cry, and yelled, "Cats! Where did they come from?! Catch those darn cats!"

Looks like we'd overstayed our welcome!

29

"So what did you guys discover?" asked Odelia.

They were driving back to town, and she was still mulling over everything that was said.

"Nothing much," said Max.

"The Harrisons bought a pony for Francine's daughters," said Dooley, "but now they don't come around anymore and the pony doesn't have anything to do and she's bored. But lucky for her she has a bird friend called Jake who tells her everything that goes on."

"Poor pony," said Max. "Has to stand there all day and nobody is riding her."

"Yeah, the mom refuses to have anything to do with her former daughter-in-law," said Odelia. "Or Francine's girls. Which is such a pity."

"Oh, and the gardener is called Chester and he doesn't like cats," said Dooley. "He even chased us but we were too fast for him—isn't that right, Max?"

"Yeah, we were too fast for the guy," Max said with a grin.

"He chased you?" said Odelia. "But why?"

"No idea," said Max. "He seems to think cats are a pest."

"Some gardeners do think cats destroy their nice lawns," she admitted. "Digging holes to do their business in."

"We would never do that," said Max indignantly.

"We might eat the grass," Dooley said. "Especially if it's nice grass. We do like a bit of nice grass, right, Max?"

"Yeah, but how much damage can one cat do? Nobody will miss a few blades of grass."

"I'm still happy he didn't catch you," said Odelia. "Some of these gardeners have pitchforks, and they don't mind using them."

"Pitchforks!" said Dooley, his voice skipping an octave. "Yikes!"

"I probably should have told them I was bringing my cats along, that way you wouldn't have been in any danger."

"Oh, dear," Max murmured.

"Max, pitchforks!" Dooley cried. "But I don't want to die by pitchfork! That sounds very painful!"

"I don't think we were ever in any danger, Dooley," said Max. "And I didn't see any pitchforks—did you?"

"No, I didn't see any pitchforks, but that doesn't mean they weren't there!"

"You made it out alive, and that's the main thing," said Odelia.

Just then, her phone chimed, and she pressed one of the earbuds into her ear, and pressed the button on the phone. "Odelia Poole speaking," she said over the noise of her ancient car's whining engine.

"Hi, Miss Poole," said a familiar voice. "This is Francine Ritter. I came to see you this morning?"

"Oh, yes, of course. I just paid a visit to your former in-laws, Mrs. Ritter."

"There's no need, Miss Poole. I just talked to Marvin Harrison on the phone, and he's agreed to pay me what his brother owed me. He'll even throw in a little bonus."

"He did? But that's great news!"

"Isn't it? I'm so happy I could cry."

"Oh, that's wonderful news."

"Thanks, Miss Poole," said Francine. "Thank you so much for all that you've done."

"I didn't do much," said Odelia, feeling much relieved. "I just had a little chat, that's all."

"Well, anyway, just thought you'd want to know."

After they'd disconnected, she thought back to her conversation with Marvin and his mother. Clearly in spite of Ruth's hard words, Marvin had managed to convince her to take a less cruel stance, and pay the mother of her grandchildren her due.

"What happened, Odelia?" asked Max.

"That was Francine Ritter. Marvin called her. He's going to pay her the back child support. Isn't that great?"

"That is great news!" said Max.

"You should ask him to let the kids play with Jane again," said Dooley. "He really needs to do that, so that Jane will be a happy pony again."

"Well, let's hope that relations will get back to normal and Ruth will invite her granddaughters over for visits again," said Odelia. Marvin looked like a decent person, and she hoped he'd continue to do right by Francine and his two little nieces.

For a moment, she lapsed into thought, and soon found her mind drifting back to the case of Franklin Harrison's death. For some reason something was still bothering her about the whole business. And suddenly she decided to have another chat with those disagreeable neighbors—the Dibbles.

"Are we going to visit the Dibbles again?" asked Max after she'd steered the car in that direction. That cat never missed a trick.

"Yeah, I thought I'd apologize on Gran's behalf," she said. "And maybe ask them again about that phone call. See, that keeps bothering me, Max."

"What does?"

"So there were three phone calls, okay?"

"Uh-huh."

"One of those calls was Gran, the other one was Joshua— so who was the third caller?"

"And you think it might have been the Dibbles?"

"It must be, right?"

"But they say it wasn't them."

"I know, but they could be lying."

Max thought about that for a moment. "Why is this so important?"

"I don't know," she admitted. "Call it a hunch."

"Your hunches are usually aces."

"Why, thanks, Max."

"So you should follow them," he advised.

She pulled up outside the Dibble place and got out. "I think this time you better stay put. The Dibbles didn't strike me as the kind of people who would love your company."

"Sure thing," said Max.

She hurried across the street and rung that now-familiar mother-of-pearl bell again. Moments later the door opened a crack, just like it had last night, and two hostile eyes bored into hers. "You again," said the woman. "What do you want this time?"

"Hi, Mrs. Dibble. I just thought I'd drop by to—"

"Bart!" the woman suddenly bellowed. "Better watch out! That reporter from last night is here again. I'll bet she's trying to distract us while her grandma burgles the place!"

"My grandmother is nowhere near here," said Odelia, who hoped that this was true. "In fact I'm here to apologize on her behalf. She should never have done what she did."

"I heard they let her out again. They should have kept her under lock and key. The woman is loony tunes. And so is her friend."

"Look, I just wanted to ask you once again: are you sure it wasn't you who called the police the night of the fire?"

"I told you this before and I'll tell you again, cause obviously you have a problem with your ears. We didn't call no cops."

"But at the police station they told me you've called the police many, many times these last couple of months. So why not when there was a fire…"

The woman's eyes flickered dangerously, and Odelia suddenly understood.

"You *wanted* that place to burn down, didn't you? That's why you didn't call the police. You hoped the place would burn down and you'd be rid of it once and for all."

"So what if we did? You can't believe the trouble we've had, missy. People coming and going at all hours of the day and night. Drug dealer central is what it was. So if you're going to ask me if I'm happy someone torched the place? Hell, yes, I am. I think whoever set fire to that dump deserves a medal."

"But three people died."

"Not people, drug dealers!"

"That's kind of harsh, don't you think? They may have been drug dealers, or drug addicts, but that doesn't mean they deserved to die."

"Nothing out here, Ma!" the woman's husband yelled. "I think this time she came alone!"

"Good," grunted the woman, and made to close the door.

"One more question," said Odelia quickly.

"Oh, what is it now?"

"So you said you saw my grandmother sitting in her car, with her friend, yeah?"

145

"So?"

"And you saw Joshua Curtis come walking out of the house. Did you see anybody else? Someone acting suspicious or who wasn't supposed to be here that time of night?"

"Look, people acting suspicious was all that place was about."

"But that particular night?"

The woman stared at Odelia for a moment, then finally said, "One person came walking from behind that fence over there. I remember thinking they looked entirely too well-dressed to be a drug addict or even a dealer."

"They?"

"Couldn't see if it was a man or a woman. Kept their head down."

"And this person came from behind that fence?" She glanced across the street. Next to the house where Franklin Harrison had died, a fence had been erected, to shield off the vacant lot which lay behind it. Graffiti covered the fence, giving it a derelict look.

"Yeah, crawled right from behind it."

"So not out of the house?"

Mrs. Dibble shook her head. "But that doesn't mean anything. There's a back entrance to number 51. Behind that fence is just an empty lot, all overgrown weeds and brush. You cross it and you're at the house. Junkies use it all the time. It's like a minefield of needles and junk. I've told the police many times to clean that place up. It's dangerous, both for pets and kids. Though no decent parent would let their kids play out there, and no pet owner on this block would ever let their dog off the leash to run around there."

"I don't understand why my grandmother didn't see this person. She was parked out here for at least half an hour before the fire."

"She wouldn't have. The person got out on the far side of

the fence and walked off in the other direction, away from where your grandmother and her friend were parked."

"So… why didn't you tell the police about this person?"

The woman was conspicuously silent for a moment, then growled, "I told you before, Miss Busybody, whoever torched that place deserves a medal, and I'm not the one who's gonna be responsible for them getting caught! If your grandma and her friend didn't see that person, I didn't see them neither—you got that? And now get lost already, will you?"

And with this, she finally slammed the door in Odelia's face.

30

*W*e were back at the precinct, and in Chase's office. Uncle Alec was out, and probably that was a good thing, as he was seemingly a little annoyed with his 'civilian police consultant.'

"So this is the second call, okay?" said Chase, who was behind his desk, with Odelia having rolled up a chair next to him. He tapped a key on his computer and the subdued voice of Joshua Curtis echoed through the room. "Then there's the third call, coming on the heels of the second one," he said, and Gran's voice sounded from the tinny speakers.

"Okay, so that was Joshua, then Gran. And how about that first call?"

Chase clicked a key and a voice spoke, but this one sounded really weird. Robotic.

"He must have used a voice changer," Chase said.

"That's some pretty sophisticated stuff, right?"

"Not necessarily. Nowadays you can easily install a voice changing app on your phone."

"So who could this person be?" asked Odelia.

"Why do you want to know? We have our man in custody, babe."

"Has Joshua confessed yet?"

"No, he's still holding out," Chase admitted. "But he's got no leg to stand on. He did it. No doubt about it."

Odelia didn't seem to be so sure. "Play that last part again, will you?"

The scrambled voice sounded through the room again. 'I wish to report a fire,' said the mystery caller. 'Parker Street fifty-one. Better hurry, or else the whole place will be gone, and I think there's still people inside.' *Click*. The call ended before the operator could ask the person for his or her identity.

"So I talked to the Dibbles again," said Odelia, "and this time Vanda Dibble admitted that she saw a person crawling out from behind the fence next to Parker Street fifty-one, hurry to their vehicle, and take off. Isn't it possible that this third person is our mystery caller?"

"Could be," Chase admitted. "But so what? Could have been a person walking their dog and seeing the fire, or someone driving past the house and doing their civic duty by calling it in."

"I don't think so. Like I said, this person came from behind that fence. There's a vacant lot that leads straight to the back door of number fifty-one. So they could have come from the house."

"Or they could have stopped to take a leak."

"Or it could be the arsonist—and our mystery caller."

Chase thought for a moment, then said, "There's no traffic cameras set up on Parker Street, but there is a traffic camera at the nearest intersection. So if you're coming from outside the neighborhood, and want to get out again, you'd have to pass that particular intersection."

"Can you access that footage?"

Chase nodded, and messed around on his computer some. Finally the screen showed some grainy black-and-white footage of the intersection in question, and so for the next fifteen minutes we all watched... nothing. No cars passing by at that time of night. And then, suddenly, a car did pass. It crossed the intersection and then in a flash was gone.

"Is that the right direction?" asked Odelia.

"Yeah, it is. They're coming from the neighborhood and driving away from town."

"Can you see the license plate?"

Chase paused the footage, then selected the part containing the license plate and blew it up and jotted down the number. He typed it into another application, looking it up in the registry. And when the name popped up on the screen, they both gasped.

"Ruth Harrison!" Odelia cried.

"Well, I'll be damned," Chase said.

"What was Franklin's mother doing out there? And, more importantly, could she be our mystery caller?"

"Why don't we go and ask her?" Chase suggested, and grabbed his coat.

§.

*A*rriving back at the house, this time with Chase behind the wheel of his squad car and Odelia riding shotgun, Odelia had that excited sensation that she was close to solving a baffling mystery.

"There's probably a perfectly good explanation," said Chase as they got out of the car and walked up to the house. "So don't get your hopes up, all right?"

When he rang the doorbell, this time it was Ruth Harrison herself who opened the door. When Chase flashed his badge, a look of fear briefly flashed across the woman's face.

"Chase Kingsley, Hampton Cove police department," he introduced himself. "And you've met Odelia Poole, my civilian consultant."

"And also your wife, or so I've been told," said the woman, quickly regaining her poise.

"Yeah, we got married last week," said Chase with a slight grin.

"Congratulations," said Mrs. Harrison as she stepped back to let them in. Once more they passed through to the sitting groom. "If you've come to talk to Marvin, I'm afraid you just missed him. He drove back into town to attend to some business."

"It's actually you we want to talk to," said Chase, not beating about the bush.

"Me?"

"Yeah, something has come to our attention that we'd like to run by you."

Odelia and Chase took a seat on the davenport, with Ruth Harrison opting for a chair.

"What were you doing outside the house where your son Franklin lived on the night of the fire, Mrs. Harrison?" asked Chase.

"What do you mean? I was never there, at that filthy place."

"If you weren't there, then how do you know it was filthy?" asked Odelia.

"People have told me these things, Miss Poole. They knew how concerned I was for the wellbeing of my son, and so they reported back to me what was going on in his life."

Chase had taken out his phone and now showed it to Mrs. Harrison. "This is a picture taken with a traffic camera at the intersection close to Parker Street 51, Mrs. Harrison.

You will note the timestamp, and also the license plate, which is clearly visible. A license plate, I might add, which is registered in your name. So I'll ask you again: what was your car doing out there, five minutes after a person using a voice changing app called 911?"

The woman stared at the picture for a moment, then finally relented. "Yes," she said. "I was driving that car. I–I didn't want to be associated with this mess, so I used a voice changer on my phone when I called in the fire. I'm sorry for lying to you, Miss Poole, but…"

"Yes, why did you lie?" asked Chase.

She folded her hands in her lap. "You must understand: even though Franklin had gone down a dark road, he was still my son, and I still loved him and wanted him to turn things around and get on his feet again. So that night I decided to pay him a visit. I'd heard he'd been kicked out of the apartment where he lived and had shacked up with a couple of his notorious friends in some squat place, so I wanted to talk to him and plead with him to change his ways. And to reconcile with his father before it was too late."

"Did you go in through the back?" asked Odelia.

"I did," said Ruth after a pause. "I thought if only I could talk to Franklin… But when I got there it was obvious there was nothing I could do. The building was on fire, so I turned back and called the police, then drove off, hoping they'd be able to save my son."

"You didn't go in?"

"N-no I didn't. There was a lot of smoke and flames. There was simply no way…"

"You didn't think to stick around until the fire department got there?"

"No. Like I said, I didn't want to be associated with this mess. I have Marvin to think about, and my husband, and of course the business, which relies very much on keeping its reputation intact. I can only imagine what the press would have made of it when they snapped a shot of me at such a notorious drug place, my dead son the addict inside."

"So you ran."

"Miss Poole, you can't understand what it's been like for us these last couple of years. And also, my husband decided to shut Franklin out of our lives for good. If he'd known I was still in touch with him, he'd have been devastated." She wrung her hands. "Though it doesn't matter now, of course."

Suddenly a young woman stuck her head in the door and announced, "The ambulance is here, Mrs. Harrison."

"Tell them I'll be there in a minute."

"Something wrong?" asked Odelia.

"My husband," said Ruth. "He died."

"Died?"

Mrs. Harrison nodded, her face suddenly a mask of grief. "Shortly after you left. I went to check on him, and found him unresponsive. He'd been ill for a long time. In fact the doctor had warned us it could be any day now."

"I'm sorry for your loss," said Odelia, and Chase murmured a few words of sympathy.

"Now if you'll excuse me, I need to bury my husband and my son." Her composure suddenly crumpled, and a lone tear slid down her cheek. "I'm sorry," she said as she touched it with the tip of her index finger. "It's been a terrible week. Probably the worst week of my life."

31

*L*ike before, Dooley and I had been left to our own devices outside. Frankly I preferred it that way. Being out and about is what it's all about, wouldn't you agree? And besides, I had some thinking to do: not just about the case, but also about the Harriet versus Shanille war that had broken out and threatened to split cat choir neatly down the middle if I didn't come up with something to stop that from happening.

We wandered over to where Jane still stood, and her face lit up when she saw us. Dooley, of course, kept an eye out for Chester's pitchfork, but so far so good.

"Hey, fellas," she said. "Twice in one day, huh? What did I do to deserve this?"

"Nothing special," I said. "Just that one of your humans seems to have gotten herself into some kind of trouble, that's all."

"Which human would that be?" she asked, interested.

"Ruth," I said. "She drove her car into town the night her son died, and forgot to mention it to the police."

"Ruth is getting old," Jane said. "It must have slipped her mind."

"I doubt it," I said dryly. "But no worries. Odelia and Chase are on the case. They'll get to the bottom of this thing. So what's happening with you?"

"Nothing much," said Jane. "Only that they're having some builders coming in soon, or so I've been told by a little birdie."

I knew we could take that literally, and said, "They're building some kind of extension? Putting in a pool, Jacuzzi?"

"Nothing of the kind," said Jane. "They're building a pagoda."

"Oh, right. We saw that."

"What they should be building is a nice new shed for me and for my companion, of course."

"Are you getting a companion?" asked Dooley excitedly.

"Not yet, but I keep hoping they will. Oh, and in other news, Mr. Harrison died."

"Yeah, we knew that already," I said. "In the fire, remember?"

"Not that Mr. Harrison. The old Mr. Harrison. Herbert. He died in his sleep just now, shortly after you left, in fact. Though I doubt whether that's got anything to do with it."

"He was old, though, wasn't he?" I asked.

"Eighty-seven or eighty-eight? Something like that? And he was pretty sick, too. I don't think he ever got over the fact that his son and heir turned down the wrong path and ruined his own life and that of his parents, too."

"Son and heir. So was Franklin supposed to take over the business?"

"Yeah, I think that was the general idea. But Franklin had other thoughts about that, obviously. And so Marvin stepped up to the plate and has done beautifully, I have to say."

"He's not married, is he, this Marvin?"

"Not yet. We're all hoping he'll find the right woman—but so far he hasn't."

"Looks like Marvin is a decent guy. He called Francine and told her he's going to pay the child support his brother owed."

"Oh, that's great. That means that maybe the girls will be allowed to visit again."

"Let's hope so."

"One ray of sunshine this week!" said Jane happily as she pawed the ground with an excited hoof. She clearly was the 'glass half full' kind of pony. "It is a little sad, though."

"What is?"

"Well, Ruth had always hoped that Franklin and his father would reconcile before the old man died, but clearly that didn't happen. And now they're both gone."

From out of the house, suddenly a young woman came hurrying. She seemed to be in some kind of a quandary, for she was muttering to herself, and making frantic gestures. She took a pack of cigarettes out of her apron and lit one up, taking anxious drags.

"What's up with her?" I asked.

"Oh, that's Elisa," said Jane. "She's a little worked up."

"Why?" I asked, my natural curiosity getting the better of me as usual.

"Slippers," said Jane.

"Slippers?" I said laughingly.

"Yeah, she's one of the maids. She takes care of the rooms amongst other things. She keeps placing Marvin's slippers on one side of the bed at night, and finds them on the other side in the morning. Guess we all have our cross to bear."

"Rich people," I said. "They're very eccentric, aren't they?"

"I find that all people are eccentric," said Dooley.

"You're not wrong, Dooley," said Jane commiseratively. "They are a strange breed."

We saw how Chase and Odelia came walking out of the house and I smiled at Jane. "Well, that's our cue," I said. "Looks like we're out of here."

"Oh, do drop by to visit again," she said. "I love nothing more than to entertain."

"We will," I promised, and then we were off, after a final wave of our tails in the direction of the hapless pony, who gazed after us with a sad look in her eyes.

"We really have to remind Odelia to plead with Mrs. Harrison to allow those kids to come back to play with Jane," said Dooley. "Maybe they could even come and live here, then Jane has someone to play with all the time."

"I'm not sure how feasible that would be, Dooley," I said. "Clearly Ruth Harrison doesn't like her daughter-in-law very much."

"But she must like her granddaughters, right? She *must* like them."

"Yeah, maybe," I said.

On our way back to town, Odelia proceeded to tell us all about the interview, and we proceeded to tell her all about our chat with Jane. All in all a very fruitful day—but still we were nowhere near proving that Joshua Curtis was innocent —if indeed he was.

"I mean, a mother would never kill her own child, would she?" Odelia argued. "So I'm inclined to believe her, Chase."

"Me, too," said Chase. "My money is still on Joshua Curtis."

"Yeah—yeah, I guess you're right," said Odelia, slumping a little in her seat. Clearly she wasn't happy that the person who'd come to her had proved a vicious killer.

"Jane said that Mrs. Harrison was desperate for Franklin and his father to reconcile," I told Odelia. "So maybe that's why she drove to that house."

"Yeah, she mentioned that. One last-ditch attempt to

bring father and son together again." She half-turned to face us. "So did you guys have a nice chat with Jane?"

"She really wants to see those girls again," said Dooley. "Can't you make that happen, Odelia—pretty please?"

"I'm not sure," said Odelia. "I'd love for that to happen, too, Dooley, but I'm afraid right now Mrs. Harrison isn't susceptible for a reunion yet."

"Or maybe she is," I argued. "Maybe if Francine Ritter goes to the funeral of her ex-husband, and her ex-father-in-law, some kind of reunion might be able to be worked?"

"Oh, yes, please!" said Dooley. "You should have seen Jane, Odelia. She's so sad. And so nice. She really needs a break."

"I'll see what I can do," Odelia said. "But no promises, all right? Mrs. Harrison is in a very vulnerable state right now."

"By the way," I said, "where was Marvin?"

"Oh, he had some business to attend to in town," said Odelia, turning back to face the front. "The future of the company rests entirely on his shoulders now."

I nodded and gazed out the window, while Odelia and Chase talked some more about the case. Something was nagging me, and if I could just put my paw on it…

And then, all of a sudden, I had it!

3 2

_F_rancine Ritter was feeling pretty great. In fact she felt that finally her life was starting to be all right again. She watched as her girls played on the living floor carpet of their cramped little apartment, and hoped that soon they'd be able to move into a different place—a better and bigger place.

She'd had to economize ever since Franklin had cut her off, her job at the supermarket not exactly paying the big bucks.

It had been such a stroke of luck for her to run into...

Suddenly the doorbell chimed and she frowned. Her girls looked up and she said, "Probably the mailman."

"The mailman, yes!" said Jaime.

"Did he bring me a present?" asked Marje.

"Yeah, I'll bet he did," she said with a smile. She loved her girls so much. She'd do anything for them—and she had. In fact she'd worked the impossible. Not exactly legal, or acceptable, but sometimes a mother had to do what a mother had to do.

She walked over to the door, and was surprised when she

put her eye to the peephole. For a moment, she hesitated, but then slid the bolt back and opened the door.

"I thought we'd arranged everything," she said as she looked into her visitor's face.

"Not quite," was the prompt reply.

❧

"We have to hurry, Odelia!" I said.

"But how can you be so sure?" Odelia asked.

"Trust me—I am one hundred percent sure. If you don't get there fast you'll have another dead body on your hands."

"Oh, dear," said Odelia, as she directed Chase to hurry along. He'd turned on the flashy blue light and was sounding his siren, too, in an attempt to stop the drama from unfolding before we got there.

"Is it the stork, Max?" asked Dooley. "Did something happen with the stork?"

"The stork is fine, Dooley," I said. "Don't worry about the stork."

"So who's in danger then?"

"We're here," said Chase, and made the car unceremoniously jump the curb.

We followed Odelia out of the car, and she said, "Maybe you guys better hang back. Things might get a little dangerous from here on out."

"Okay, fine," I said, and watched Odelia and Chase hurry up to the door of the apartment building. It wasn't much of a dwelling, more like one of those slightly run-down places that probably shouldn't be allowed to still accept tenants.

The moment Chase and Odelia disappeared inside, I told Dooley, "Let's go."

"But I thought we were supposed to hang back?"

"When have you ever known us to allow our human to enter the lion's den without us being there to keep an eye on her, Dooley?"

"Um… never?"

"Exactly. So let's not let her down now. Whether she likes it or not, we're her guardian angels."

"I thought we were feline angels?"

"That, too."

So we hurried inside, and started up the stairs.

"Where are we going?"

"I think I remember Odelia telling Chase it was the third floor."

We pretty much zoomed up those stairs. Don't let my slightly chunky appearance fool you. I can be pretty fast when I need to be. In fact we arrived there even before Chase and Odelia did. Probably the elevator was as ancient and run down as the entire building. As luck would have it, the door to the apartment was ajar, so we rushed right in. In the living room two little girls were playing, and from the adjoining room I heard choking sounds, so we moved right on through, and found Marvin Harrison, his hands around Francine Ritter's throat, busily choking the life out of her.

So Dooley and I did what we do best in such circumstances: I launched myself at the man's neck, while Dooley dug his claws into his left hand, and his teeth into his right.

Marvin screamed like a banshee, and immediately let go of his victim. For the next few moments he whirled around like a drunken sailor, one cat attached to his neck, and the other attached to his hands. When finally we were forced to let go, Chase was there, gun in hand, and quickly made the man lie flat on his belly, hands out, to make the arrest.

Francine, meanwhile, was being comforted by Odelia. The poor woman's throat was red and swollen, but it looked like she'd be all right.

And Dooley and myself? Thanks for asking! I'm happy to announce that we were just fine. I'd been swung into a corner of the room, making a hard landing, but had escaped with my life, and Dooley had landed on the bed and was now calmly licking his claws, removing all evidence of the foul killer we'd just taken down in a concerted effort.

"He tried to kill me," said Francine hoarsely. "The bastard tried to kill me!"

"I know," said Odelia. "Try not to talk, honey."

"Marvin Harrison," said Chase as he placed handcuffs on the guy's hands, "I'm arresting you for the attempted murder of—"

"That's not Marvin," I told Odelia. "That's Franklin. And Chase should probably arrest him for the murder of his brother Marvin, too, and the murder of those other two men."

Odelia gaped at Marvin/Franklin. "Franklin?" she asked.

The guy turned to her, and flashed a nasty grin. "So you finally figured it out, huh?"

Odelia turned to me, then to Francine. "But…"

"Yeah, that's Franklin, all right," said Francine. "I recognized him immediately. He might have fooled all the others, but he didn't fool his own wife—I know my husband."

"Oh, shut up—you ruined everything!" Franklin yelled as Chase escorted him out of the room, then past his kids, and out of the apartment.

"I don't understand," said Odelia. "I thought that was Marvin."

"He must have taken his place," said Francine, gingerly touching her throat. "Don't ask me why, though knowing Franklin it must have something to do with money."

"We better get you to a doctor to have that looked at," said Odelia.

"My girls," said Francine. "I don't want them to see me

like this." She threw Odelia a pleading look, and Odelia quickly searched around, found a scarf, and helped Francine tie that around her neck.

Then we all left the bedroom, and Francine announced to her girls, "We're going on a little trip, girls. Do you want to come?"

They both cheered and said, "Yeah!"

Then they caught sight of us, and turned their attention to the two 'pussy cats.'

I must admit that being fondled by a three-year-old did not become me. They poked us, and they prodded us, and pulled our ears, all the drive down to the doctor's office!

When finally we arrived at our destination, and Odelia helped Francine out of the car, followed by her two girls, Dooley turned to me and said in a shaky voice, "Max, maybe when that stork finally arrives, we'll simply pretend like we didn't see it?"

I smiled at my friend. "Had enough already, have you?"

He nodded emphatically. "They pulled my ears, they pulled my tail, they poked my belly, they even tried to poke my eyes, wanting to know if they were real! Max, I don't want babies. Ever!"

"That's fine, Dooley. Neither does Odelia—at least for the time being." I glanced down the street, and said, "And now let's solve this other little matter, shall we?"

"What other little matter?"

"The big rift."

33

*S*hanille was walking down the street, on her way to the General Store to talk to Kingman and ask him to join her effort to oust Harriet from the group once and for all, when suddenly she was accosted by Max and Dooley.

"Hey, you guys," she said. "Fancy meeting you here." She grinned, indicating this was one of her little jokes. Unfortunately Max wasn't smiling, and neither was Dooley, for that matter.

"Shanille, we need to talk," said Max.

"Just what I was thinking. We need to have a nice long talk about Harriet."

"Of course," said Max, gracious as ever. "And we will. But first I would like to talk to you about the new cat choir Dooley and I are starting."

"The new cat choir?" she asked, much surprised.

Max nodded. "Frankly Dooley and I have had it with these fights between you and Harriet, so we've decided to start our own cat choir, and I'm sorry to tell you that you are not invited, Shanille. And neither," he added when she opened her mouth so speak, "is Harriet, for that matter."

"This will be a choir without you and without Harriet," Dooley said, making matters perfectly clear.

"But... you can't do that!" said Shanille.

"We can and we will," said Max. "And I'll have to be honest with you, Shanille, we've been talking to a lot of the other cats about this, and they're all very excited about this new project. In fact every single cat we've talked to so far has agreed to come on board."

"They're all fed up with all the fighting," Dooley said.

"Yeah, this will be non-fighting cat choir. A cat choir where all the members join up strictly to have a good time, to sing together, have fun together, and to shoot the breeze. To gossip and to crack jokes and enjoy the kind of warm friendship that we all like."

"And you're not invited," Dooley repeated, "and neither is Harriet. Right, Max?"

"Absolutely. So far we're looking at, oh, eighty-five to ninety percent of the cats?"

"You've already talked to ninety percent of my members?"

"Something like that. And all of them—"

"That's one hundred percent," Dooley added.

"All of them have signed up. So it looks like very soon now there will be three cat choirs: the one run by me and Dooley, the one run by you, which will have only one single member, and the one run by Harriet which also will have but a single member."

"Too bad, but that's just the way it is," said Dooley.

"But that's not fair!" said Shanille. "I want to have a cat choir where cats get together to have a good time, and sing and have fun together!"

"Well, I guess you had your chance and you blew it," said Max with a shrug.

"But Max, please—you can't do this!"

"I'm afraid we just did," said Dooley.

"But… can't I join your cat choir, Max? Please?"

Max looked at Dooley, and Dooley looked at Max, then Max said, "I'm afraid we can't do that, Shanille. Because if we let you in, we also have to let Harriet in, and you know what that means."

"There will be fighting," said Dooley. "That's what Max means."

"I won't fight, I promise. It's Harriet who's the trouble. She's the one who's always fighting. Undermining my authority and picking fights."

"See?" said Max to Dooley. "This is why I told you not to allow Shanille in."

"You told me this would happen," said Dooley, nodding sagely.

"Exactly. So no, Shanille, we won't let you in. I'm very sorry."

"But…" She thought hard. "But what if I make up with Harriet? What if I talk to Harriet and the two of us make up and promise to be friends? Would that work?"

"I'm not sure," said Max dubiously.

"I'm not sure either," said Dooley. "Would it?"

"You'd have to make up with Harriet first," said Max. "And you'd have to convince us that you mean it."

"I will—I promise you I will!"

"Do you believe her, Dooley?" asked Max.

"I want to believe her," said Dooley.

"Look, talk things over with Harriet, all right? And better sit out cat choir tonight. And when you feel like you're ready, you and Harriet better convince us that you mean business. Or else it's bye-bye with cat choir for you. Is that understood?"

She nodded fifty times in quick succession. "Absolutely."

"I think she understood, Max," said Dooley.

Max smiled. "I think so too, Dooley."

166

Shanille walked off, and thought hard about what Max and Dooley had told her. She didn't want to leave cat choir. Cat choir was her life. If they kicked her out… And so she went in search of Harriet. She needed to patch things up with her—pronto!

૬& a

*H*arriet had been planning and plotting, plotting and planning, with Brutus in her wake. Her mate wasn't as excited about the prospect of her running cat choir as she was, but that couldn't be helped. Part of joining the ranks of upper management was that one was supposed to be able to motivate the lower echelon, and so she'd been working on motivating Brutus, but so far her pep talks hadn't had a lot of effect on the black cat.

"When I'm in charge of cat choir I'll basically run this town," said Harriet as they walked along the sidewalk in the direction of the General Store to convince Kingman to join her side. "And you know what that means, Brutus."

"No, I don't know what that means," said her life partner.

"It means all the perks are ours!"

"What perks?"

"The perks—you know."

"No, frankly I don't know. And frankly I think antagonizing Shanille also means antagonizing half this town's cat population."

"Only if I don't succeed in convincing the majority to vote for me," she said.

"What if fifty-one percent does vote for you? Then forty-nine percent will still be against you. There will be two cat choirs. One run by you and one run by Shanille. And it's going to make life in this town a living hell for us, can't you see that?"

No, she didn't see that. What she did see was that she had to beat Shanille. The choir conductor had annoyed her one time too many and she had to go. No matter the consequences.

Suddenly, out of the blue, Max and Dooley materialized in front of them, blocking their passage.

"Hey, guys," she said. "I was just looking for you. You are going to vote for me tonight, aren't you? You know how important this is."

"I'm afraid we have some bad news for you, Harriet," said Max.

"Bad news for you, good news for us," said Dooley.

"What bad news?" asked Harriet, looking from Max to Dooley.

"We're starting our own cat choir," said Max.

"And you're not invited," said Dooley.

"What?!" she laughed. "What are you talking about?"

"We've decided that we've had enough of all the bickering, and we're starting our own bicker-free cat choir," said Max. "And you're not in it, and neither is Shanille."

"But…" She blinked and glanced to Brutus for support. He just stood there, a slight smile on his lips, the traitor! "You can't do this!"

"Funny. That's exactly what Shanille said," said Max.

"Yeah, she said just the same thing," Dooley added.

"You talked to Shanille already?"

"She wasn't happy," said Dooley.

"You know that she actually said she'd talk to you and try to reconcile?" asked Max.

"Shanille wants to talk to me and reconcile?"

"She begged us to be included in our new cat choir," Max explained, "and we told her the only way that was ever going to happen was if she promised that you and she would get along from now on."

"Shanille and me getting along?"

"Yeah, crazy, right? We all know you and Shanille will never get along. And so one hundred percent of the cats we've talked to so far—"

"Which represent ninety percent of the Hampton Cove cat population," said Dooley.

"—have agreed to join our new cat choir, on the condition that you and Shanille are not allowed in as members. So there you have it. From now on there will be three cat choirs in town: ours, yours, and Shanille's."

"But you guys!"

Brutus now started laughing for real. "I love it," he grunted.

"Brutus, shut up!"

"Sugar plum, you know I love you, but I'm sick and tired of all the bickering, too. If you and Shanille can't get along, maybe you should start your own cat choir, with only the two of you as members. That way you can bicker and fight as much as you want, and you won't stop the rest of us from having a good time."

"But…" She looked from Max to Dooley to Brutus. "But but but…"

"Oh, there's Shanille now," said Max. "Well, I guess we'll just leave you to it. But remember: the only way you can join our new cat choir is if you promise to behave."

"But Max!"

But Max was off, followed by Dooley and… Brutus!

And then it was just Shanille and her.

Both cats stared at each other for a moment in awkward silence, sizing each other up, then Shanille said, "I guess they told you about their new cat choir?"

"Yeah, they just did."

"And the fact that either we get along or we're both out?"

"Yeah, can you believe that? I mean, you *are* cat choir, Shanille. Cat choir is nothing without you."

"Oh, I don't think so. Cat choir is bigger than either of us, Harriet. Cat choir isn't me, or you, or any of us. Cat choir is the whole community—all the cats of Hampton Cove. And frankly if they really decide to kick us out…"

And for the first time ever, Harriet saw that Shanille actually had tears in her eyes!

"Oh, sweetie," she said. "Don't be sad. We'll just go to Max and talk to him together."

"I know Max, Harriet. He isn't kidding. I can tell."

Yeah, frankly she'd had that impression herself. Max usually was such a laidback individual, but when things got rough he could be really tough. There had been a note of steel in his voice when he'd explained the rules of new cat choir to her, and he'd meant what he said: either they patched things up, or no more cat choir for either of them.

"Look, I think maybe we let things get a little out of hand," she said finally.

"You think?" Shanille scoffed.

"But you can be so annoying, Shanille!"

"Oh, as if you're not annoying, *Harriet*!"

They both glowered at each other for a few beats, then burst out laughing.

"What are we doing?!" Harriet cried.

"We're idiots, both of us!"

"I'm the biggest idiot of all, though."

"No, I'm the biggest idiot."

"No, Shanille—*I'm* the biggest idiot!"

"Okay, fine. You win. You're the biggest idiot, and I'm the second-biggest idiot."

"Fair enough," said Harriet, much sobered.

They were both silent for a moment, then Shanille said, "So how do you want to play this?"

"I say we go to Max and tell him that we reconciled."

"Did we reconcile, though?"

Harriet gave her frenemy a warm smile. "Of course we did. Shanille, you know there's no one I love to fight with more than you."

"Aw, do you really mean that?"

"Absolutely. You're my absolute favorite nemesis in the world."

"And you're my favorite nemesis."

"But maybe we won't tell Max about that part, all right?"

"No, I don't think he'd understand."

Somehow, though, Harriet had a feeling that he would.

EPILOGUE

"*O*kay, so spill, Max," said Harriet. "Tell us how you figured it out, cause I gotta be honest with you—I do not understand anything!"

"Me neither," Brutus grunted.

"It's those two girls," said Dooley.

"What two girls?"

"Jaime and Marje. They pulled my tail and they pulled my whiskers, and then they pulled my ears and poked my belly, and so I said no more. No more babies. So no more stork either. Isn't that right, Max?"

"Absolutely, Dooley," said Max, "though I don't think that's what Harriet was talking about."

"Oh."

"Odelia!" said Gran. "You have got to explain what happened, cause I don't understand a thing!"

"Me neither," Uncle Alec grunted irritably as he nursed a cold brewski.

We were in Marge and Tex's backyard, with Tex manning the grill as usual, and providing us all with those delicious nuggets of grilled meats and veggies we all love and adore so

172

much. Okay, so some of them were medium rare while others were rare, and still others were overdone, but let's not nitpick. The fun of a barbecue is not the quality of the food, but the quality of the people present, right? And the quality of those present was nothing to be caviled at: the entire Poole clan, of course, expanded with Charlene and Scarlett. And on the cat side there was of course myself, Dooley, Harriet and Brutus.

"Okay, so what do you want to know?" I asked.

"Everything!" said Harriet. "Just take it from the top, Max, and don't skip anything!"

"Fine," I said. "So Franklin Harrison had come to the end of his rope, right? And he knew there was no way for him to redeem himself. His dad had cut him off, and had cut him out of his will, and so he was effectively stuck. Now you have to remember that this was a man who hadn't worked a day in his life, and he didn't intend to start working for a living now. And so he decided there was only one way out of this: by getting rid of his twin brother and making it look as if he was the victim. That way he could take Marvin's place, and suddenly the bad twin had become the good twin, and he had the world at his feet again. I don't have to explain to you that Franklin is not a good person. Never was."

"He probably squished ants when he was little," said Dooley.

"Only problem was," said Odelia, who was telling the same story but to the human audience, "that he needed a fall guy, right? Someone to blame the murder on. And who better to blame than that loser Joshua Curtis, who'd been hounding him ever since he'd been foolish enough to start something with Melanie Myers? So Franklin set up a meeting with Joshua at the Parker Street house and arranged the rendezvous for eleven forty-five on the night of the murder, so making sure that the house wouldn't have burnt down completely, and that Marvin's body would still be more or less unblemished."

"See, he didn't want the police to have to check the victim's teeth," I explained.

"Because that would have been a dead giveaway," said Odelia. "They'd have known the victim wasn't Franklin Harrison but was in fact Marvin Harrison. This was also the reason he made sure his brother's lower torso and arms were seriously burned—he wanted to make sure that no fingerprints could be lifted from the dead person."

"He'd already left by the time Joshua arrived, sneaking out the backdoor and through the vacant lot next to the house. He was seen leaving by Vanda Dibble, but that couldn't be helped. And then to make sure that the fire department would get there on time, he called 911 himself and masked his voice with a voice changing app. He then drove straight across town to Joshua's house and planted the jerrycans in his garage. He knew the way, since he'd been there before to steal a glass from Joshua's kitchen, hoping it would contain the man's fingerprints. He then placed his own fingerprints, added some Rohypnol mixed with a little water, and made sure to plant the glass at the scene."

"But," said Gran, "how could he be sure that his brother would die from smoke inhalation? Wasn't that leaving things to chance?"

"It was," said Odelia. "Which is why he killed Marvin somewhere else."

"He actually killed his brother in that old shed we saw on the family domain, Dooley," I said. "Remember how that was partially burned out? He arranged to meet his brother, drugged him, then set the shed on fire and waited until Marvin was dead from smoke inhalation. Then he removed him from the shed and transported him to Parker Street, where he arranged the scene to make it look as if Marvin had been killed in the fire."

"It's a miracle Vanda Dibble didn't see him arrive at the scene," said Marge.

"Oh, I'm sure she did," said Odelia. "She saw what she figured was just another drug dealer arrive, and unload what she assumed was a big shipment of drugs. She didn't report it to the police, since she'd reported that kind of thing so many times before, and she'd lost faith in the police department."

"Raiding that place was on my list," Uncle Alec muttered. When Charlene rubbed his arm, he added apologetically, "It's a long list."

"I know, honey," said the Mayor. "And you are under-staffed. And I will make sure you get more people so that this sort of thing won't happen again."

"So he killed his brother, and then what?" asked Tex, who'd joined them at the table, tongs in hand, allowing the meat on the grill to sizzle merrily—though perhaps a touch too long.

"Well," said Odelia, "now he had to take his brother's place and pretend to be him. Now you can fool the people who only know you superficially, but it's a lot harder to fool your own family."

"I think Franklin's mom figured it out almost immediate-ly," I said, "but he told her he and Marvin met and Marvin died in a freak accident, and he was too late to save him."

"And how did he explain that he'd decided to take his brother's place?" asked Brutus.

"That's where Ruth made a big mistake," I explained. "She should have called him out on that, but she didn't. And it's understandable, of course. Franklin had always been her favorite son—the son she loved the most, even though he was the most mischievous one. And I think she was so happy to see him return to the bosom of the family that she decided to overlook the ruse. Maybe she even thought it wasn't such a bad idea, seeing as how Marvin's death would have meant a great disruption for the business side of things, since her husband would have adamantly refused to accept Franklin suddenly taking over at the helm of the company."

"And then Herbert Harrison suddenly and conveniently dies," said Chase.

"I don't think that was an accident," said Odelia. "I think Franklin killed his dad. Pushed a pillow down on his face and smothered him. He hasn't confessed to that yet."

"But he will," Chase grunted.

"But why?" asked Harriet.

"Isn't it obvious?" I said. "The old man must have realized that Franklin had taken the place of his brother, and he wasn't going to accept that. He also must have suspected that Franklin killed his brother—he knew what kind of man his son was. So Franklin decided to end things for the old man, and grab the reins of the family business free and clear."

"How horrible," said Marge, shaking her head.

"Yeah, he's a real piece of work," Odelia agreed.

"So what about Francine Ritter?" asked Gran. "Why did he try to kill her?"

"Because she recognized her husband the moment she saw him. She wasn't fooled. And he knew that would happen, which is why he refused to see her. But then they happened to meet on the street, and that was it. Francine knew it was him, and quickly put two and two together, and decided to use the opportunity to finally make him pay. And he promised he would, until he decided he wouldn't—and tried to kill her."

"God," said Scarlett. "What a terrible business."

"But how did you find out, Max?" asked Harriet. "How did you figure it out?"

"Well, two things," I said. "First there was the shed, and then there were the slippers."

"The shed and the slippers? That sounds like a Disney movie."

"So when we visited the Harrisons we saw that little shed that was half burned down. At first I thought this must have happened a long time ago, but then Jane—she's the pony who used to belong to Francine's girls—told me how the gardener was such a marvel. How he always kept the place looking so immaculate. So it got me wondering why a gardener like that would tolerate that decrepit old shed? And of course he didn't. That fire happened a couple of days ago, when Franklin murdered Marvin. And then he decided to have it torn down to remove the evidence, and build a pagoda in its place."

"And what about the slippers?" asked Brutus.

"One of the maids had expressed her bewilderment at how she put Franklin's slippers on one side of the bed at night, and how in the morning she always found them on the other side. A man can change identities, but he just might forget on which side of the bed the twin he murdered used to get up in the morning."

"But how did you know he was going to try and kill Francine Ritter?"

"I remembered how frightened Franklin had looked just after meeting Francine on the street. I'd figured at the time he was afraid that now he'd have to pay her the child support his brother owed, but why would a man of such wealth be afraid of a measly sum like that? No, he was scared, all right —scared because he knew that Francine had recognized him, and that as long as she was around, his secret would never be safe."

"And so he tried to make sure she'd never talk again," said Brutus, nodding.

"What a story," said Harriet. "And what a good thing you figured it out in time, Max. Or else those two girls would be orphans now."

"Francine and her girls are going to move in with Ruth Harrison, by the way," I said. "She's finally realized that her former daughter-in-law didn't have a bad influence on Franklin, but that Franklin was actually the debilitating influence in her life."

"So Jane is going to have her friends back?" asked Dooley happily.

"Yes, Dooley," I said with a smile. "Jane will finally have her friends back, and Ruth will finally get to spend more time with her granddaughters—in fact she'll be spending all of her time with them, as she's looking for a CEO to run the business from now on."

"See?" said Gran. "I knew that Joshua was innocent. Odelia's clients always are."

"Joshua was never my client, Gran," said Odelia, pressing her point again. "I'm just a reporter, and reporters don't have clients. We only have stories to pursue."

"Well, this sure was one hell of a story," said Marge. "Anyone more potato salad?"

And while Marge ladled more potato salad onto everyone's plates, Charlene gave Uncle Alec a little shove. "Well?" she said when he didn't react. "Wasn't there something you wanted to say?"

"Um…" said the Chief, scratching his scalp. "Well, I'm afraid I've acted like a fool, Odelia. I thought you were hampering my case, while in fact you were solving it. So…"

"That's all right, Uncle Alec," said Odelia magnanimously. "You don't have to apologize."

"Actually I'm the one who should apologize to you, Chief," said Chase. "Even though you told me not to, I kept feeding Odelia information from the investigation."

"I knew you did," Uncle Alec grumbled. "But that's all right. If you hadn't, Francine Ritter would be dead right now, and Joshua Curtis would still be in jail—an innocent man." He sighed deeply. "Maybe I'm getting too old for this stuff."

"Nonsense," said Charlene curtly. "You just need to learn to listen to your niece. She's a smart cookie. But since the apple doesn't fall from the tree, you're a smart cookie, too, all right?"

"More like hardtack," he said with a grimace.

"And you owe me an apology, too, by the way," said Gran. "Scarlett and I did the right thing trying to get rid of that evidence, isn't that so, Scarlett?"

"Um, not too sure about that, Vesta," said Scarlett.

"Yeah, not too sure about that either," said the Chief with a not-so-apologetic look at his mother and her friend. "Next time you pull a stunt like that I'm keeping you two overnight. Is that understood?"

"Yes, Alec," said Scarlett meekly.

"Yes, Alec," Gran said, equally meekly, after getting a full dose of her son's irritation.

"So how is cat choir?" asked Odelia as she joined us, and came bearing gifts in the form of a few little prize nuggets of meat she'd saved from total annihilation for us.

"Cat choir is just grand," said Harriet. "Shanille and I have made up, and Max has decided to let us into his new cat choir, isn't that right, Max?"

"Yeah, but you know the conditions, Harriet."

"What are the conditions?" asked Odelia with a smile.

"No more fighting!" said Brutus and Dooley in unison.

"Sounds like a great idea," said Odelia, and gave us all cuddles and kisses, then whispered into my ear, "You did great, Max. And what's even better: you made me look good, too. So thank you for that."

"I couldn't have done it without you, Odelia," I said. Which was absolutely true.

"We make a great team, don't we, buddy?"

"Yes, we do."

Suddenly Dooley raised his eyes, and started saying, "Shoo! Shoo! We don't want you here, stork! Shoo!"

"That's not a stork, Dooley," I said. "That's a pigeon."

"Oh, phew," he said, and sank down onto the porch swing again, not meeting Odelia's eye.

"Dooley, for the last time, Chase and I are not going to start a family just yet. Okay?" She gave him an extra cuddle. "You guys are my family. And right now you're all I need."

And wasn't that the best endorsement any cat could hope to get from their human?

Dooley leaned over to me and whispered, "Do you think I should take down that 'Stork, go home!' sign now, Max?"

"Yeah, I think that's probably a good idea, Dooley," I whispered back.

THE END

Thanks for reading! If you want to know when a new Nic Saint book comes out, sign up for Nic's mailing list: nicsaint.com/news

EXCERPT FROM PURRFECT RUSE
(MYSTERIES OF MAX 33)

Chapter One

Look, don't get me wrong: I enjoy a murder even less than the next cat, even though it isn't necessarily my own species who's affected by this tragic loss of life. But when the only cases coming Odelia's way are spouses wanting to catch their other spouses in the act of cheating on those selfsame spouses—the first spouses, not the second ones, if you see what I mean—life becomes pretty dull and monotony soon reigns supreme.

Dooley, though, didn't seem to mind all these people being cheated upon—or is it cheated on—from finding their way into Odelia's office. But then again, Dooley watches a lot of daytime soaps, and eighty percent of the storylines on these soaps are just the cheating kind of stuff. The other twenty percent is probably illegitimate children suddenly popping up out of the blue, which frankly speaking is the same thing.

So it was with a sigh of relief that I greeted the next person entering our human's office at the Hampton Cove

Gazette. She was a large woman with red-rimmed eyes, clearly suffering from some acute or life-threatening trouble. Immediately I assumed murder, which just goes to show how warped my mind has become after having spent the formative years of my life in Odelia's presence and that of her cop husband, her cop uncle and her neighborhood watch grandma. And it was with bated breath that I pricked up my ears as the woman took a proffered seat and launched into her tale of woe.

"My Chouchou has gone missing," she lamented.

"Murder," I told Dooley, my friend and housemate who was lounging right next to me in the cozy little nook of the office Odelia had reserved for us. "Just you mark my words, Dooley. Chouchou is this woman's husband and he's been murdered."

"Strange name for a husband," said Dooley.

"Who is Chouchou?" asked Odelia, not missing a trick. She had looked up from her computer where she'd been busily typing up a report of her recent visit to the town library, where a recital by some local children's orchestra had taken place.

"My sweet baby," said the woman, sniffling and pressing a Kleenex to her eyes.

"Not a husband, a kid," I corrected my earlier statement. "Bad business, Dooley. A child killer on the loose."

"Strange name for a kid," was Dooley's opinion.

"And when has Chouchou gone missing?" asked Odelia.

"Last night," said the woman, waving a distraught hand in the general direction of the street. "She usually goes out at night but by the time I get up in the morning she's always lying at the foot of the bed, sleeping peacefully. Only this morning she wasn't there!"

"Does your daughter always sleep at the foot of the bed?" asked Odelia with a curious frown. It isn't up to her to judge people, so she never does, but she couldn't hide her surprise at this strange way to spend a night.

"Oh, but Chouchou isn't my daughter," said the woman. "She's my little gii-ii-ii–rl!"

"So is Chouchou a… dog?" Odelia guessed.

The woman promptly stopped wailing, and gave Odelia a look of surprise. "Of course she's not a dog. She's my precious sweetheart. My sweet and lovely Maine Coon."

"Huh," I said, sagging a little as a sense of slight disappointment swept over me. Cats going missing is not exactly the kind of case I live for. Cats go missing all the time, you see, and usually they show up again within twenty-four hours, when their sense of adventure is sated and they return, utterly famished and happy to be home again.

"So Chouchou went missing last night," said Odelia, summing up the state of affairs succinctly. I could see she was less than excited at the prospect of traipsing all over town in search of a missing cat. "So does Chouchou usually stay out all night?"

"She does, but like I said, she's always back in the morning. I have no idea where she goes, and frankly I don't care—live and let live, I say, and that goes for my pets, too."

"Pets as in… you have more than one cat?"

"I have a gerbil," said the woman.

"Gerbils aren't pets," I muttered.

"So what are they?" asked Dooley.

"Pests," I returned.

"Look, you come highly recommended, Miss Poole," said the woman, who still hadn't given us her name, by the way. "Everybody knows that you're Hampton Cove's leading cat lady, and so if there's anyone who can find my precious baby it's you." She leaned forward, a pleading look in her eyes. "Can you help me find my Chouchou—please?"

"If I were you, Miss…"

"Bunyon," said the woman. "Kathleen Bunyon. And it's Mrs."

"If I were you, Mrs. Bunyon, I'd wait another twenty-four hours. I'm sure that your baby will show up as soon as she gets hungry."

"But this is not like her. She never stays out this long. Can't you please help me?"

"Did you go to the police?"

"I did. And you know what they said?"

"I can imagine."

"They said missing pets are not a priority at the moment. Can you imagine? If a missing pet isn't a priority, what is?"

"Missing people, perhaps?" I suggested.

The woman glanced in my direction, having picked up my discreetly mewled commentary. "Oh, I see you bring your babies to work with you. Very clever."

"Yeah, they like to be where I am," Odelia confirmed with a warm smile.

Suddenly Mrs. Bunyon got up and joined me and Dooley in our corner. "Can't you find my baby for me, sweet pussies? I know you're as clever as Miss Poole is—or at least that's what people keep telling me."

I turned to Dooley. "Do you know this Chouchou?"

"I'm not sure," said Dooley, thinking hard.

"What does she look like?" I asked.

And if you think it's strange for two cats as established in our local community as we are not to know all the cats that reside in that community, I have to confess that there are so many cats now that it's frankly impossible to know them all. Furthermore, not all cats are as socially active as Dooley and myself are, so the name frankly didn't ring a bell.

"What does your Chouchou look like?" asked Odelia, as she opened a new file on her computer and started typing.

"Well, she's small and very beautiful. Oh, wait. I've got a

picture of her on my phone." Mrs. Bunyon took her phone out of her purse and swiped it to life. "In fact I have more than one," she admitted, and started showing us a regular barrage of pictures. She must have had thousands on there. All of them showed a very hairy Maine Coon, with a slightly stunned look in her eyes, as if she hadn't signed up for the life of a photo model.

"Nah," I said. "Never seen her before in my life."

"You have no idea where she goes at night?" asked Odelia.

"Not a clue," said Mrs. Bunyon as she pressed play on a video she'd shot of her fur baby playing with a sponge. "The neighbor says he sees her walking in the direction of the park when he walks his dog, and that's usually around eleven o'clock at night."

"Cat choir," I said knowingly.

"I haven't seen her either," said Dooley, who'd taken a long time to come to a definite position on this. "If she's a member of cat choir she's one of the less noticeable ones."

Not every member of cat choir likes to stand out, of course. Some of them like to be the star of the show, like Harriet, our Persian housemate, but others simply show up and stay in the background.

"Look, I'll see what I can do," said Odelia with a pointed look in my direction.

I rolled my eyes. "Really?" I said. "She's probably just wandering around having the time of her life. She'll be back before you know it."

"Don't you worry, Mrs. Bunyon, I'll find your Chouchou for you" said Odelia, widening her eyes at me.

"Oh, all right," I said with a groan. "I'll go look for her. But if she's home safe and sound while we're traipsing all over town looking for her..."

"The moment she arrives home you'll tell me though, right?" said Odelia.

"Oh, yes, of course." Mrs. Bunyon had clasped her hands together in a gesture of silent prayer. "You'll find her for me, won't you, Miss Poole? You'll do whatever you can to bring my baby home to me?"

"Yes, absolutely," said Odelia, making a promise I knew she was going to hand over to me as soon as Mrs. Bunyon had left—it's called delegating and humans are experts at it.

"Thank you," said Kathleen Bunyon. "Thank you so much!" She'd clasped Odelia's hand and squeezed it, then vigorously shook it, almost removing it from its parent socket. "I knew I could count on you."

The moment the woman had left, Odelia gave me and Dooley a smile. "Looks like you've got your work cut out for you, boys," she said, then pointed to the door. "So chop, chop. Don't dawdle. Go and find Chouchou."

"We're not dogs, Odelia," I said with an exaggerated sigh as I got up from my perch.

"I know you're not dogs, but you saw how devastated Mrs. Bunyon is over the disappearance of her cat. And just imagine if you guys went missing, how devastated I would be."

"We'd never do that to you, Odelia," said Dooley earnestly. "If we went missing we'd first tell you where we went missing to."

"Come on, Dooley," I said. "Let's go and find ourselves a Chouchou."

Chapter Two

Traipsing along the sidewalk, I must confess at that moment I had no idea the mess we'd soon find ourselves in. As I said, cats go missing all the time, and in due course they always come back. So I had no reason to assume that this time things would be different.

"Where are we going, Max?" asked Dooley.

"Well, let's first talk to Kingman," I suggested. In our town Kingman is also the king of gossip. I'm not sure if that's why he's called Kingman, but he is the cat we all turn to when we need to find out what's going on in our local little feline community.

Kingman is a very large and frankly slightly obese cat, who likes to hold forth outside his owner's grocery store, where he enjoys both an endless supply of cat food, courtesy of Wilbur Vickery, his human, and an equally endless supply of pretty lady cats prancing by. Kingman isn't just the king of gossip, you see, but also something of a ladies' cat.

"Max! Dooley!" he said by way of greeting. "Just the fellas I wanted to see!"

"Hello, Kingman," I said as I returned his hearty greeting. "What did you need us for?"

"I've got a favor to ask you. See, Wilbur wants back in."

"Back in what?"

"Back in the neighborhood watch, of course. He's been reading about how Vesta has been so successful dealing with this recent crime wave, catching bad guys all over the place, and he wants a piece of the action." He lowered his voice as he darted a quick look at his human, busily ringing up wares for his never-ending line of customers. "Wilbur is bored to his eyeballs. And he fondly remembers his time, however brief, as a member of the watch. He feels he's not doing enough for this town so he wants back in. So what do you say?"

"What do you want me to say?" I said, not sure what it was that Kingman expected from me.

"Talk to Vesta! Tell her to let Wilbur back on the team!"

"You know Vesta, Kingman. She'll never go for it."

"Come on, Max, don't be like that. You hold sway with

the woman. If you ask her to let Wilbur back on the team, I'm sure she'll give it some serious consideration."

Frankly I wasn't sure that letting Wilbur back on the watch team was such a good idea. The last time he'd been a member he'd made a real nuisance of himself.

"Oh, and you better ask her to let Francis Reilly back in, too."

"Father Reilly wants back in, too?"

"Sure! You know that he and Wilbur are like this." He intertwined twin nails to show us how close the shop owner and the parish priest were. It was an unlikely friendship, I must admit, since Wilbur isn't exactly a paragon of virtue. More like a paragon of vice, the way he likes to ogle any person of the opposite sex, whether eligible or ineligible.

"Look, I'll talk to Gran, all right?" I said. "But first you've got to help us, Kingman."

"Ask me anything! Frankly, between you and me, if Vesta doesn't take Wilbur back, that man is going to drive me nuts. All he does all night is sit on his couch and whine!"

"Look, a cat has gone missing," I said, wanting to get off the topic of Wilbur and onto the topic I was really interested in.

"Her name is Chouchou," Dooley supplied helpfully. "And she's a Maine Coon."

"She's a member of cat choir but after last night's rehearsal she didn't come home."

"Probably out on a toot," said Kingman knowingly. "You know how it is. A couple of us like to hit the town after cat choir, and this Chouchou of yours must be just like that."

"She didn't sound like a party-loving cat to me, Kingman," I said.

"More like a peace-and-quiet-loving cat," Dooley added.

"What does she look like?" asked Kingman with a slight frown.

"White with red stripes across her face."

"She's very pretty," said Dooley. "In an understated sort of way."

"Very pretty, eh?" said Kingman, rubbing his whiskers thoughtfully. "Mh."

Kingman knows pretty. In fact I'm willing to bet that Kingman probably knows every cat who scores more than a five or a six on his personal prettiness scale.

"I think I know the cat you're talking about," the large cat finally said. "Chouchou. Yeah, definitely rings a bell. Mousy kind of feline, right?"

"Chouchou is not a mouse, Kingman," said Dooley with a laugh. "She's a cat!"

"Yeah, even a cat can be mousy, Dooley."

"They can?" asked Dooley, much surprised.

"Sure. Just like a mouse can be catty, a cat can be mousy."

"Huh," said Dooley with a frown as he processed this startling new information.

"So have you seen her or haven't you seen her?" I asked, wanting to get to the bottom of this missing cat business and move on. I'd been enjoying a leisurely time in Odelia's office and wanted to return to my cozy little nook posthaste if you please.

But Kingman shook his head. "Can't say that I have," he said. "You see, Chouchou is not one of those cats that really stand out, if you know what I mean."

"You mean she's more like a cat who stands in?" asked Dooley.

"Not exactly," Kingman replied with a grin. "And besides, you know how it is—cats go missing all the time. But they always come back."

I didn't enjoy my own line being quoted back to me, and I grimaced at this.

"And it's not as if Chouchou is the only cat that's gone

missing lately. In fact I know of at least half a dozen who've suddenly disappeared. But do I look worried?"

Dooley studied Kingman closely. "You don't look worried, Kingman," he determined.

"And that's because I'm not worried! Because cats always land on their feet!"

"So you have no idea where she could be?" I asked, not hiding my sense of disappointment. Usually Kingman is a fount of information, but today he was more like a fount of frustration, with his pleas to let Wilbur Vickery and Father Reilly back on the neighborhood watch, something I was pretty sure Gran would be dead set against.

"Sorry, fellas," said Kingman as his eyes wandered in the direction of a petite Siamese who'd come walking along. "Can't help you." And it was clear our audience with Hampton Cove's unofficial mayor was at an end when he called out, "Trixie! Long time no see!"

So we decided to move on and soon were treated to a rare sight: our very own human, putting up flyers on lampposts, depicting the very cat we were looking for.

Chapter Three

Odelia had decided that the best thing she could do was to print out some flyers of Mrs. Bunyon's missing cat and distribute these around Hampton Cove. And she'd just started doing this when she came upon her grandmother, who was sipping her usual hot cocoa in the outside dining area of the Star hotel, along with her friend Scarlett Canyon.

"I've got a job for you, Gran," said Odelia as she placed a little stack of flyers in front of both ladies. "A cat's gone missing, and I want you to put up these flyers for me."

"Missing cat?" asked Gran with a frown as she glanced at the flyer. "I'm sorry, honey," she promptly added as she handed the little stack back. "The watch doesn't do missing cats."

"You're not serious."

"Of course I'm serious. The watch takes care of the big stuff—serious crime. Missing cats is not something we've got time for, I'm afraid."

"Vesta, we could look into this one missing cat for Odelia," said Scarlett, who was dressed to the nines in a nice little floral top, her red hair done up and her makeup tastefully applied. "I mean, it's not like we've got anything else going on at the moment."

"No, but we could have something else going on soon, and if we're locked into this cat business we won't have time for the other, more important stuff, now would we?"

"Just... do it already, will you?" said Odelia, who didn't want to waste time standing around arguing with her recalcitrant grandmother.

And she placed the flyers in Scarlett's hands, who took them gratefully, and said, "Don't you worry about a thing, honey. We'll take care of this for you."

"Scarlett!" said Gran. "What are you doing?"

"Missing cats are part of the watch's mission statement, or didn't you get the memo?"

"What memo? What mission statement?"

Scarlett grinned. "Okay, so there's no memo, but I think finding missing pets definitely should be part of our mission statement."

"Oh, all right," Gran grumbled. "But if the big one hits and we're too busy looking for this... Chouchou of yours, I'm going to blame you."

Just then, Max and Dooley came trotting up. "We just talked to Kingman," said Dooley, "and he says at least half a dozen cats have gone missing, but he's not worried, because cats always land on their feet."

"Half a dozen cats?" said Odelia.

"What did he say?" asked Scarlett.

"That more cats have gone missing," said Gran.

"At least half a dozen," Dooley reiterated. "But he's not worried and so neither should we. Isn't that right, Max?"

"Absolutely," said Max, though the large blorange cat did look slightly worried.

"Kingman thinks that these missing cats went on a toot and they'll be back soon."

"Cats don't go on toots," said Odelia with a frown.

"What did he say?" asked Scarlett, trying to read Dooley's lips and failing.

"That Kingman says the missing cats have gone on a toot."

"Do cats go on toots?"

"No, they don't. Cats don't drink," said Gran. "So correct me if I'm wrong, but if half a dozen cats have gone missing, shouldn't the police be out looking for them?"

"The police aren't interested in missing cats," said Scarlett. "They've got better things to do—just like you, by the way, Vesta."

Gran had the decency to pull a remorseful face. "Okay, so maybe you were right."

"Can you please repeat that?" asked Scarlett, placing her hand to her ear.

"You were right, all right?!"

"This is a momentous occasion," said Scarlett, giving Odelia a wink. "Vesta Muffin admitting she was wrong."

"I didn't say I was wrong. I just said you were right. There's a difference."

"Oh, and Kingman says Wilbur and Father Reilly want to rejoin the watch," said Max.

"No way in hell," Gran growled.

"What did he say?" asked Scarlett, starting to look a little frustrated.

"Wilbur and Francis want back on the watch."

"No way in hell," said Scarlett, a rare frown marring her smooth brow.

"That's what I said!"

"So what do you want us to do?" asked Max. "About Chouchou, I mean?"

"I want you to keep looking," Odelia instructed. "Meanwhile I'll drop by the police station and see if they've received any of these missing cats reports. If they all went missing around the same time we just might have a catnapper on our hands."

"A catnapper!" Dooley cried.

"Better ask the people from the shelter, too," said Gran. "They may have hired some overzealous newbie, who goes around picking up any and all pets that are roaming free."

"But I don't want to be napped!" said Dooley, much disturbed. "I don't think I'd like it."

"You're not going to get taken, Dooley," said Max reassuringly. Then, turning to Odelia, he added, "We're on the case. If those cats were nabbed, we'll find them for you."

Gran shook her head. "People kidnapping cats. What is the world coming to?"

ABOUT NIC

Nic has a background in political science and before being struck by the writing bug worked odd jobs around the world (including but not limited to massage therapist in Mexico, gardener in Italy, restaurant manager in India, and Berlitz teacher in Belgium).

When he's not writing he enjoys curling up with a good (comic) book, watching British crime dramas, French comedies or Nancy Meyers movies, sampling pastry (apple cake!), pasta and chocolate (preferably the dark variety), twisting himself into a pretzel doing morning yoga, going for a run, and spoiling his big red tomcat Tommy.

He lives with his wife (and aforementioned cat) in a small village smack dab in the middle of absolutely nowhere and is probably writing his next 'Mysteries of Max' book right now.

www.nicsaint.com

ALSO BY NIC SAINT

The Mysteries of Max

Purrfect Murder

Purrfectly Deadly

Purrfect Revenge

Purrfect Heat

Purrfect Crime

Purrfect Rivalry

Purrfect Peril

Purrfect Secret

Purrfect Alibi

Purrfect Obsession

Purrfect Betrayal

Purrfectly Clueless

Purrfectly Royal

Purrfect Cut

Purrfect Trap

Purrfectly Hidden

Purrfect Kill

Purrfect Boy Toy

Purrfectly Dogged

Purrfectly Dead

Purrfect Saint

Purrfect Advice

Purrfect Cover

Purrfect Patsy

Purrfect Son

Purrfect Fool

Purrfect Fitness

Purrfect Setup

Purrfect Sidekick

Purrfect Deceit

Purrfect Ruse

The Mysteries of Max Box Sets

Box Set 1 (Books 1-3)

Box Set 2 (Books 4-6)

Box Set 3 (Books 7-9)

Box Set 4 (Books 10-12)

Box Set 5 (Books 13-15)

Box Set 6 (Books 16-18)

Box Set 7 (Books 19-21)

Box Set 8 (Books 22-24)

Box Set 9 (Books 25-27)

Box Set 10 (Books 28-30)

The Mysteries of Max Shorts

Purrfect Santa (3 shorts in one)

Purrfectly Flealess

Purrfect Wedding

Nora Steel

Murder Retreat

The Kellys

Murder Motel

Death in Suburbia

Emily Stone

Murder at the Art Class

Washington & Jefferson

First Shot

Alice Whitehouse

Spooky Times

Spooky Trills

Spooky End

Spooky Spells

Ghosts of London

Between a Ghost and a Spooky Place

Public Ghost Number One

Ghost Save the Queen

Box Set 1 (Books 1-3)

A Tale of Two Harrys

Ghost of Girlband Past

Ghostlier Things

Charleneland

Deadly Ride

Final Ride

Neighborhood Witch Committee

Witchy Start

Witchy Worries

Witchy Wishes

Saffron Diffley

Crime and Retribution

Vice and Verdict

Felonies and Penalties (Saffron Diffley Short 1)

The B-Team

Once Upon a Spy

Tate-à-Tate

Enemy of the Tates

Ghosts vs. Spies

The Ghost Who Came in from the Cold

Witchy Fingers

Witchy Trouble

Witchy Hexations

Witchy Possessions

Witchy Riches

Box Set 1 (Books 1-4)

The Mysteries of Bell & Whitehouse

One Spoonful of Trouble

Two Scoops of Murder

Three Shots of Disaster

Box Set 1 (Books 1-3)

A Twist of Wraith

A Touch of Ghost

A Clash of Spooks

Box Set 2 (Books 4-6)

The Stuffing of Nightmares

A Breath of Dead Air

An Act of Hodd

Box Set 3 (Books 7-9)

A Game of Dons

Standalone Novels

When in Bruges

The Whiskered Spy

ThrillFix

Homejacking

The Eighth Billionaire

The Wrong Woman

Made in the USA
Monee, IL
25 February 2021